True love comes once in

When Kathryn Abbott mov
her divorce, she doesn't exp ... *Brett Falcone, the*
Italian Stallion. If possible, he's even more appealing than he
was twenty years ago when she, the nerd queen, tutored the
popular baseball star.

Brett would like to begin the relationship they couldn't have
then, but first Kathryn must face her past decisions...and risk
losing the love of her life all over again.

ALSO BY HELEN HARDT

Follow Me Series:

Follow Me Darkly

Follow Me Under

Follow Me Always

Darkly

Wolfes of Manhattan

Rebel

Recluse

Runaway

Rake

Reckoning

Billionaire Island (Wolfes continuation)

Escape

Gems of Wolfe Island (Wolfes continuation)

Moonstone

Raven

Garnet

Buck (coming soon)

Non-Fiction:

got style?

PRAISE FOR HELEN HARDT

WOLFES OF MANHATTAN

"It's hot, it's intense, and the plot starts off thick and had me completely spellbound from page one."
  ~The Sassy Nerd Blog

"Helen Hardt...is a master at her craft."
  ~K. Ogburn, Amazon

"Move over Steel brothers... Rock is *everything!*"
  ~Barbara Conklin-Jaros, Amazon

"Helen has done it again. She winds you up and weaves a web of intrigue."
  ~Vicki Smith, Amazon

FOLLOW ME SERIES

AUTHOR'S NOTE

Welcome to the Helen Hardt Vintage Collection! These are the back list of my back list—stories that I wrote at the beginning of my career that were either never published or published long ago.

Reunited is now part of the HH Vintage Collection!

Reunited was originally published by Musa Publishing in an anthology called *Love Notes* in 2012. It was then published as a standalone also by Musa when the anthology when out of print. I published the novella independently in 2019 through my own publishing house, Hardt & Sons. However, it truly belongs in the vintage collection.

I love the new cover, and for those who haven't yet read *Reunited*, please enjoy it!

To everyone who believes in second chances.
Happy Holidays!

1

My flesh tingled, my tummy tightened, and my heart made a mad dash to leap from my chest. My fingers, seemingly of their own accord, pushed the button to replay the message I'd just heard.

"I'm calling for Mr. or Mrs. Abbott. My name is Brett Falcone, and it looks like Maya's going to be on my soccer team. Practice will start next Monday at six o'clock..."

I let the words fade.

Brett Falcone.

His voice had deepened just a little, but it was him—the man from my past I thought I'd never see again. Yet that glimmer of hope, that flicker of desire, had always burned within my heart.

I hadn't known he was still in town. Of course I'd only been back a few months. After my divorce from Danny, I'd moved back to my hometown of Columbus, Ohio. Danny still lived in Cleveland, close enough that Maya could see him on the weekends.

Twenty years ago, I'd left Columbus and vowed never to return. I met Danny in California ten years later. Five years after that, when he received a job offer in Cleveland, I'd agreed to return to Ohio. Cleveland was far enough away from Columbus that I didn't have to think about my former life of heartbreak and humiliation.

When my marriage had crumbled, though, Columbus had seemed like the place to pick up the pieces. *Sometimes*, I'd said to myself, *you just want to go home.*

Home.

Amazing how, even after twenty years of telling myself I'd never set foot in Columbus again, it still felt like home. The townhome I'd rented had grown on me, and I enjoyed my pediatric practice at a local clinic. I'd even made a few friends, though I hadn't contacted anyone from my high school days. I couldn't.

Brett Falcone.

For twenty years I'd tried to erase him from my memory.

For twenty years I'd been unsuccessful.

What could I do? Call the county sports association and ask that Maya be put on a different team? Maybe. I couldn't withdraw Maya from soccer. She was only four, and she was excited about her first chance to play a team sport. I couldn't take that away from my daughter.

I checked my watch quickly. Four thirty. My mother was picking Maya up at the sitter's and taking her for the night. Danny would pick her up tomorrow morning and take her for the rest of the weekend. I had nowhere to go. Though it was Friday, someone would likely still be at the sports registration office until five. I shuffled the papers on my desk until I found the copy of Maya's registration and keyed in the number.

"Tri-County sports."

"Yes, hello. This is Kathryn Abbott. My daughter is registered for Pee Wee soccer, and I was wondering if there was any chance we could change her to a different team."

"I'm sorry, ma'am. All the teams are full. We didn't have as many volunteers for coaching, so there aren't any open slots. Unless you'd like to coach a team?"

I arched my brows. Avoiding Brett Falcone might be worth learning soccer. Unfortunately, I had no athletic talent whatsoever. The sheer unfairness of all this! Brett Falcone would be a great coach. He was a natural athlete, great at soccer and football. But his first love had been baseball.

"Ma'am?"

I jolted back to reality. "I'm sorry. No, I can't coach, though I wish I could. I know nothing about soccer, about any sports. I really want my daughter to learn. To do what I never had the talent to do."

God, I was babbling. The teenybopper on the other end of the line didn't care about my lack of sports experience.

"Then I'm afraid I can't help you."

"I understand. Thank you for your time."

I set the phone back on the cradle.

Brett Falcone.

The Italian Stallion.

How he'd lived up to that name.

I poured myself a glass of iced tea and sat down in my recliner. I took a long sip of the crisp beverage, letting it float over my tongue and coat my throat. Then another. I needed to cool off. Just the name Brett Falcone had made my entire body blaze like an inferno.

I set the tea down on an end table, leaned back, and closed my eyes.

Brett Falcone.

Twenty freaking years. Well, in three days, I'd see him again.

What would happen?

I had no idea.

～

Twenty years earlier

"You wanted to see me, Mr. Phillips?"

"Yes, Kathryn." The guidance counselor motioned for me to enter his office. "Close the door and have a seat."

I complied. I'd never been in a counselor's office. I was a straight A student, editor of the school newspaper, member of the orchestra, president of National Honor Society. I'd received early admission to Stanford, my dream school. Spring was here, the school year was nearly over, and graduation was just around the corner. Why was the senior guidance counselor summoning me? What had I done wrong?

I sat, quiet, and waited for him to tell me.

He cleared his throat. "I suppose you're wondering why I called you in here."

"I haven't done anything wrong, have I?"

He smiled. "No, of course not. You're a model student."

I heaved a sigh of relief. "Thank goodness."

Mr. Phillips chuckled, shaking his head, and part of his comb-over fell over one ear. "You weren't really worried about that, were you?"

"No. Not really, but you never know."

He nodded. "I called you here because I need your help, Kathryn."

"Of course. What do you need?"

"We have a student who needs a tutor. I think you might be the best fit."

"Oh? Who is the student?"

"Brett Falcone."

"The Italian Stallion?" I clamped my hand on my mouth. Not the thing to say to the senior guidance counselor.

Mr. Phillips, however, let out a laugh. "Yes. The Italian Stallion. He's failing math, Kathryn. If he doesn't get his grades up, he can't play baseball. Our team needs him."

"You're kidding, right? I don't mean to be disrespectful, but you want me to tutor Brett Falcone so he can play baseball? Why are sports so important, Mr. Phillips? Why isn't it important that he learn math because it's math? Math is a lot more useful in life than batting a ball."

I was overreacting, but still I seethed. The emphasis schools put on athletics angered me. I'd never been good at sports, was always the last picked for any team in gym class, and I'd revered the day, sophomore year, when I finished the last required physical education class of my high school career. No doubt all the jocks and jockettes had revered that day too. No longer would they be saddled with the class nerd on any of their teams.

"Normally, I'd agree with that assessment," Mr. Phillips said, "but he's already been offered a scholarship to play baseball at OSU. If he doesn't get his math grade up, he won't keep the scholarship."

"A scholarship?" I shook my head.

Brett Falcone would never make it in college. Clearly, he was barely making it through high school.

"So you want me to tutor him and get his math grade up so he can play in college?"

Mr. Phillips cleared his throat again and his cheeks reddened. "Yes, that's correct."

"I think I might be too busy. I have my own grades to think of, you know. And the newspaper and—"

"We all know you've already been admitted to Stanford. Your grades at high school level no longer matter."

I opened my mouth, but Mr. Phillips held up his hand.

"You're an incredibly gifted young lady, Kathryn. Your grades won't suffer for helping another. You know that as well as I do."

"Be that as it may, Mr. Phillips, I cannot help Brett Falcone. He and I have a…history."

"A history?"

Mr. Phillips's bulgy eyes bulged out even farther. No doubt he was wondering what kind of history the Italian

Stallion could possibly have with Kathryn Zurakowsky, nerd extraordinaire.

"Yes."

"May I ask what kind of history?"

"Not a good one, and nothing I care to talk about."

"How would you have a history? You don't run in the same crowds. Do you even know Brett?"

Did I know Brett Falcone? *Know* was such an innocuous word. It didn't describe my relationship with Brett Falcone. Granted, once we'd gotten to high school, he'd left me alone. Middle school, though, had been hell on earth, courtesy of the Italian Stallion.

But Mr. Phillips didn't know that, and I had no desire to enlighten him.

"I'm afraid I have to decline," I said. "I'm sure you can find another tutor for Brett."

"Kathryn, there isn't anyone else who can tutor him."

"That's ridiculous. How about Leon Bates? He's as good in math as I am. Seth Connors might even be better. Or do you want a female tutor? How about Mary Beth Rogers? She's pretty good. Or Amy Eckard."

"All fine students," Mr. Phillips said, "however none of them are acceptable."

"Why not?"

"Because"—he sighed—"Brett refuses to work with anyone but you."

I widened my eyes. "Me? That's the silliest thing I've ever heard. Brett hasn't said a word to me in four years."

"Believe me, I'm as flabbergasted as you are." Mr.

Phillips nodded. "But Coach Henderson said Brett would only agree to a tutor if it was you."

My jaw dropped open. What in the world was Brett Falcone thinking?

"Well, it just so happens that I don't give a hoot whether Brett Falcone gets to play baseball in college, so the answer is no."

"Kathryn"—Mr. Phillips rose and came around to face me—"there's more at stake than that."

"Oh?"

"His family has suffered a setback. His father was injured on the job a few weeks ago."

"I'm very sorry, but—"

"A scholarship would be a great help to Brett and his family. Otherwise, if Brett doesn't go to school, he'll probably have to get a job and help support his family."

"Maybe that's his lot in life."

"Maybe so. But he can have so much more. Brett Falcone is not stupid. I shouldn't be telling you this, but he scored in the 'superior' range in the state-administered tests. The boy just needs some guidance, some hope for a future. You can help him."

"And if I don't?"

"Then you'll have to live with that."

"Mr. Phillips, I'm quite capable of living with that." I stood and turned to walk out the door, but Mr. Phillips's voice stopped me cold.

"Kathryn. *Please*."

2

————

His strong legs looked exactly the same.

My pulse raced, but I steadied myself as I led Maya toward the Pee Wee soccer field. Brett stood with his back to us, talking to another parent. He was wearing sports shorts and a T-shirt, coach fare. His jet-black hair still fell to his collar in unruly waves.

My stomach knotted. How was I going to get through this?

I looked down at my adorable daughter, so cute in her shin guards and cleats.

Maya. That's how I'd get through this. For Maya.

Once I was within speaking distance, I cleared my throat. "Mr. Falcone?"

He turned, and I melted into a puddle. Age had been kind to the Italian Stallion. Streaks of silver threaded through the silky hair at his temples. Dark stubble graced his jaw line. His dark brown eyes still appeared black, and the lashes were still long and thick. Those lips—once firm and supple upon my own—were still red, full, and gorgeous.

And his athlete's body? Oh, yeah, there it was. I remembered as though it were yesterday instead of twenty years ago. That flat belly, those strong virile arms, the corded neck, the hard and muscled chest.

He looked at me, cocked his head, as though he were trying to place me.

I held out my hand, willing it not to tremble. "I'm Kathryn Abbott, and this is Maya."

His gaze pierced mine, and I knew the second recognition hit.

"I'll be damned. Kathryn Zurakowsky."

I smiled, my lips quivering. "Abbott now. How are you, Brett?"

"Can't complain. You?"

I nodded. "Life's been good. How did you end up coaching?"

"My daughter's playing. That's her, with the dark hair." He motioned to a little girl kicking a soccer ball across the field.

I nodded and raked my gaze over his left hand that hung at his side. No wedding band. But he had a daughter on this team, so he must be married. He probably just took off his ring to play soccer. Made perfect sense.

"So this is Maya, huh?" Brett knelt down. "Hi, Maya. I'm Coach Brett."

"Hello," Maya said shyly.

"I know your mommy from a long time ago."

"When she was little like me?"

"Not quite *that* long ago." Brett laughed. "Are you excited to play soccer?"

"Oh, yeah!" Maya clapped her hands together.

"I'm hoping she got her father's athletic talent," I said. "As you'll recall, I don't have any."

Brett ignored my comment. "You ready to start kicking a ball, Maya?"

"Sure!"

"Okay, then." He took her hand. "Mommy'll stay here, and I'll take you to meet the rest of the girls on the team."

I smiled. "Go ahead, Maya. I'll be right here reading my book while you have your practice."

I set up my folding chair, sat down, and opened my romance novel. After reading the same paragraph five times, I still had no idea what it said.

I looked up. Brett had set up orange cones and was showing the six little girls how to kick the ball around the cones. His demeanor was kind, paternal. I couldn't imagine Danny doing something like this. He'd be too authoritative and demanding. Danny was a gifted athlete, or had been, when he was younger, but I doubted he was coaching material. At least not for this age.

Brett had no doubt married his high school sweetheart, Michelle Bates. That had been his plan at the end of high school anyway, whether or not the scholarship came through. Bubbly, blond Michelle was probably the mother of the little dark-haired beauty on the field. Or maybe Brett had divorced Michelle and married again. For him to have a child so young, that was definitely a possibility. Or maybe he and Michelle hadn't worked out and he'd only married more recently, like I had.

Whatever the case, I couldn't sit here ogling him for another fifteen minutes. Thank goodness soccer practice for four-year-olds only lasted half an hour.

I pretended to read my book for the remainder of practice. Finally, Brett brought the girls together in a circle and made them join hands in the middle. "Blue thunder on three," he said. "One, two three."

"Blue thunder!" a chorus of happy little girl voices cheered.

Maya ran to me.

"Did you have fun, sweetie?"

"Oh, yeah, it was tons of fun. I love to kick the ball!"

"Then you're in the right sport." I laughed as I folded up my chair and stuffed it in its bag. I wanted to be well on my way before Brett was done talking to the pretty young woman hanging on his every word. Must be another parent. A very young and attractive parent. Of course she'd be young. Most parents with children Maya's age were in their twenties, not thirty-eight like I was. And Brett, for that matter.

I slung the chair over my shoulder. "Grab your ball, Maya."

Maya picked up her size-three soccer ball and smiled up at me. "Ready, Mommy."

"Let's go then. I promised you a milkshake, didn't I?"

"A milkshake sounds great."

I turned toward the deep timbre. Brett had heard me?

"I think Zoe might like a milkshake. Do you mind if we join you?"

He had to be kidding. "Well...no, of course not."

"We can go over to The Robin's Nest and the girls can have a milkshake and play on the tot lot. You and I can catch up."

My cheeks warmed.

"That would be fun, Mommy," Maya said. "Zoe's real nice."

Nice to be put on the spot. I couldn't talk to Brett. I just couldn't. So much history. Too much unresolved between us.

"Please, Mommy?" Maya tugged on my sleeve.

I had a hard time saying no to Maya these days. The little girl missed Danny so much. Divorce was hell on a kid, but I wouldn't be doing my child any favors by letting her have everything she wanted. I wasn't going to have one of those spoiled children of divorce.

"I have an early day tomorrow, sweetie. I'm sorry."

"Oh, Mommy, please! You did promise me a milkshake."

So I had. I sighed. "You're right. I did. If Coach Brett and Zoe want to join us, that would be wonderful."

"Oh, good!" Maya jumped away from me and grabbed Zoe's hand. "My favorite's vanilla. What's yours?"

"Strawberry," the other girl said.

"I remember your favorite, Kath." Brett's breath warmed my neck. "Chocolate. Right?"

My skin bristled. No one else had ever called me that.

My mom called me Kathy. Everyone else, including Danny, had always called me Kathryn.

Kath.

Brett's husky timbre trickled over me like thick, dark chocolate. My knees weakened. I remembered. Remembered exactly how he'd licked chocolate off my warm neck...

The warmth of a flush drifted over my flesh. "I stopped eating chocolate when I was pregnant with Maya," I said, my voice shaky. "I couldn't stand it during morning sickness."

Actually, I'd stopped eating chocolate years before, after I left town. I'd stopped eating it for a reason I wasn't ready to think about right now. Maybe not ever.

"Really?" Brett stepped beside me. "I'm surprised. I remember you as a true chocoholic."

"Things change," I said.

"You okay?"

"I'm fine. It's... It's good to see you again, Brett."

"I didn't realize you were back in town."

"I've only been here a few months."

"You kind of dropped off the face of the earth, you know."

"Yeah." I cleared my throat. "I had my reasons. You did marry Michelle, didn't you?"

He nodded. "Yeah, I did."

"That's what I figured." I shifted my gaze to Maya and Zoe skipping ahead.

Twenty years earlier

MY THROAT CONSTRICTED as I walked into Mrs. Knott's math classroom. I'd refused to see Brett in my home or his for tutoring, so Mr. Phillips had arranged for our use of a classroom after school. I shook my head. What was the world coming to? To go to such effort just for baseball seemed fruitless to me.

Brett, to my surprise, was already in the classroom. I'd hoped we'd be chaperoned by Mr. Phillips or a teacher, but that wasn't possible. However, the principal and Mr. Phillips would be in the building until five, so if I needed them, I could contact them via the intercom. Not that I feared for my physical safety around Brett. No, he wasn't like that. Especially not with me. I just didn't want to be alone with him for reasons of my own.

"Hey there," he said.

"Hi." I whisked through the maze of student desks quickly and took a seat at the teacher's desk. Why not? I was the teacher, right?

"Can't you sit beside me?"

"No. You're here to learn. I'm here to tutor you. That makes me the teacher, you the student."

He let out a drawling guffaw. "If you say so, teach."

"Cut the attitude," I said. "I'm here to help you, and according to Mr. Phillips, you wanted me and no one else."

"True."

"So treat me with respect, or I leave."

The muscles in Brett's perfectly sculpted face tightened. I'd hit a nerve. Interesting. But why? Why did he insist on me as a tutor when several other just as qualified individuals existed who didn't share our history?

Of course, maybe he didn't even remember our history. He'd left me alone for the past four years. He was one of the beautiful people, the popular crowd. He probably didn't remember how he'd tormented me, made my middle school years hell, been the cause of many tears shed into my pillow.

Not that I ever let him see me cry. No, I was too proud for that. I'd always waited until I got home to my empty house before letting the dam break.

No time for that now. I was bound to tutor Brett Falcone, and the sooner we started, the sooner we could finish.

"What exactly do you need help with?" I asked. "Mr. Phillips said you're failing math."

"Dummy math."

"Intro to Algebra?" I shook my head.

Brett Falcone was an asshole to the nth degree, but I'd never thought he was stupid. Not a genius, to be sure, but failing Intro to Algebra? Something else was at work here.

"I didn't know seniors could take that class. Isn't it a Freshman class?"

"Not for us dummies."

"All right, enough of that talk. It's counter-productive."

He laughed. "What the hell does that mean?"

"It means if you keep telling yourself you're a dummy, you'll become one. So shut up already."

"Yes, ma'am." He saluted me.

"Ha-ha. Okay, where are you having the problem?"

"First, let me ask you a question."

"Sorry. I'm the tutor here. I ask the questions."

"No, I'm the student. I'm the one with questions."

He had a point.

I blew a strand of hair out of my face. "What's your question?"

"Why did you agree to tutor me?"

"That's not a mathematical question, Brett."

"No. But I'd like to know."

I huffed. "Fine. If I answer that, I get to ask you a question."

"Fair enough. So why?"

"Mr. Phillips made me an offer I couldn't refuse."

"What offer?"

I wasn't about to tell Brett that our counselor was paying me out of his own pocket. I took it because I needed the money. I had a full scholarship for my tuition to Stanford, but I still needed money for housing and food. "None of your business. I answered your question, now you answer mine."

"You didn't answer mine."

"Oh, yes, I did. It was a perfectly acceptable answer to the question as posed. Next time, ask a more specific question." I couldn't help a slight smile. "Now, why did you insist on me for a tutor?"

"You're the smartest person I know."

"You haven't said two words to me in four years. How do you know I'm the smartest?"

"You've always been the smartest, Kath. Since we were

little kids." His lips curved into a churlish grin. "And there's another reason."

"Which is?"

"You're a fox."

I caught my chin before it dropped to the floor. A fox? This from Brett Falcone, the boy who'd tormented me for being an ugly nerd? Granted, once the braces had come off and I'd gotten contact lenses, my looks had improved. My mother told me I was beautiful, but she was my mother, for God's sake. No one else had.

"I'd much rather look at you for an hour than one of those other nerds."

Heat crept up my neck. Damn! I didn't want him to see that his words affected me. This was Brett Falcone, the boy who'd made my life miserable, the boy who'd made me cry. What did I care if he found me attractive now? He was probably lying anyway. He wasn't a nice person.

"Looking at me won't get you the C you need."

"But studying with you will."

"Let's get one thing straight right now." I raked my fingers through my feathered hair. "We aren't studying together. I'm teaching, and you're learning. There's nothing magical about sitting here with a student who knows math. You aren't going to learn through osmosis, Brett. You need to take an active part in this process."

"Yeah, yeah. Whatever."

I stood and gathered my books. "I'm leaving."

I was halfway to the door when a warm hand gripped my elbow. A spark shot through me.

"Please. Don't go. I need you. Really."

I turned. This would be so much easier if he weren't so damn good-looking. Every teenage girl's fantasy. "You've got a funny way of showing it."

"I'm sorry. Most girls like it when I tell them they're pretty."

"Most girls didn't get tormented by you in middle school."

His high cheekbones reddened. Had I actually embarrassed him?

"I was hoping you didn't remember that."

"Not remember that?" I shook my head. "You really think I can forget being told I'm ugly on a daily basis? Being made fun of in gym class at every opportunity? Being tripped in the hallway?" I closed my eyes and inhaled. Deeply.

Never let them see you cry.

I opened my eyes and met Brett's dark gaze straight on.

He bit his bottom lip. "I didn't think you cared. You never said anything."

"Oh. So you would have stopped if I'd given a damn? If I'd cried my eyes out for you? Is that what you wanted?"

"No. I mean..." He sighed. "Aw, hell. I don't know what I mean. I was a punk, okay? A stupid kid. I honestly didn't think I was hurting you. I honestly didn't think you cared. I'm sorry."

An apology from Brett Falcone? What was more, it even sounded sincere. For a moment, elation speared through me, until I realized he needed me. He was just trying to get me to tutor him so he could get his grade up and play freaking baseball. That's all this was. A forced apology. An act.

I could act as well as the next person. "Fine. You're right. I didn't care, and I don't care now. Frankly, I don't care if you flunk out of high school and never play baseball again. But I made a deal with Mr. Phillips, and I, unlike you, am a person of honor and integrity. I keep my bargains. So I accept your apology. Now let's get down to business."

Brett took a seat and smiled. Though I didn't want it to, my gaze gravitated to his full red lips, his perfect white teeth, that cute dimple on his left cheek. The heavens had wasted so much charm and good looks on this young man. If only he had a kind heart to go with it all.

"You *are* a fox, you know," he said.

I rolled my eyes. "If you say so. Now, tell me what you're working on in class."

3

"They seem to get along well," Brett said, as he handed me a vanilla milkshake.

Zoe and Maya had already clambered to the tot lot. Brett carried the girls' and his own shakes to a table. He waited for me to sit before he sat down across from me. Always the gentleman, Brett Falcone. That had surprised me when I first found out.

"So how is Michelle?" I asked, taking a sip of the thick shake.

"She's good."

"I'm glad to hear it."

"We're not together anymore."

I swallowed quickly to avoid choking on the creamy, smooth shake. "Oh. I'm sorry."

He nodded. "Thanks. But it's okay. We drifted apart over the years. Our two older girls are nineteen and seventeen. We thought having Zoe would save our marriage." He shook his head. "It didn't."

I didn't know what to say, so I took another sip of shake.

"Not that I regret having Zoe. She's been great for both of us, and for Candy and Marie."

"Those are your older girls?"

"Yeah. They adore her. And Michelle has a new lease on life. We were both so young when we had Candy and Marie. We're definitely better parents now, even if we aren't together."

"You never remarried?"

"The divorce was only final about a year ago. I haven't really dated. Haven't really wanted to. It's weird when you've really only dated one person your whole life."

That comment sliced into my gut. Then again, he was right. Brett and I had never actually dated. "I see." Another sip. My hands seemed conspicuous. What could I do with them?

"How about you? How long have you been married?"

"I'm not," I said. "Maya's father and I separated last year. When the divorce came through, I relocated back here."

Was that a smile trying to escape his beautiful lips? I wasn't sure. Wasn't sure I wanted to know.

"What do you do, Kath? I always imagined you'd do something absolutely great with your life."

"I'm a pediatrician."

"Wow. I bet you're fantastic at that."

I let out a chuckle. "I try. It's very rewarding most of the time. Heartbreaking sometimes, though."

"I can imagine."

"How about you? What are you doing?"

"Construction, like my dad did."

"Did you end up going on that baseball scholarship?"

"Only for a year. I couldn't stay in school. Michelle got pregnant, and there were other circumstances."

"I'm sorry." My heart plummeted to my stomach. All I'd hoped for him had never happened. "I wish you could have finished."

"Me too. Believe it or not, I actually liked college, Kath. I think I have you to thank for that."

My skin tingled as warmth crept to my cheeks. "You don't owe me any thanks. You were always intelligent. You just didn't know it."

"You told me I was, and I believed it."

"If I hadn't told you, someone else would have."

"*You* did. No one else did."

Again, I had no idea what to say. I took a long loud sip of my shake and turned my head to watch the girls playing. They were laughing as though they'd known each other for ages. But that was the way of it with little girls. They could become best friends in an instant.

"There's something I've always wondered, Kath."

I turned to face Brett's dark, burning gaze. "What's that?"

"Why did you leave?"

I swallowed the lump that formed in my throat. "I had a scholarship to Stanford. You know that."

"Yeah, I knew that. But you didn't go to Stanford."

"Of course I went to Stanford."

"Not right after high school."

Embarrassment burned up my neck, my face. How did he know? "I took a year off."

"Why? No one knew where you'd gone. I tried to get in touch with you. Your mother wouldn't tell anyone where you were."

"I asked her not to."

"Why?"

"Why did it matter? You were all set to marry Michelle."

"I almost didn't."

I jolted. "What do you mean?"

"I tried for months to find you. And the night before my wedding, I went to your house. I begged your mom to tell me where you were."

"Why would you want to find me? You were pseudo-engaged to Michelle throughout all of high school."

He pulled his wallet out of his back pocket, opened it, and took out a yellowed piece of paper. He handed it to me.

"I wasn't in love with Michelle, Kath. I was in love with you."

◠

Twenty years earlier

"THANK YOU."

Had my ears deceived me? Or had Brett Falcone just thanked me?

"You're welcome." I forced the words out. "Same time next week?"

"Tomorrow, actually."

"Brett, I don't have time to tutor you tomorrow. It's Friday. I have...an engagement."

"An engagement?" He laughed. "You sound so businesslike."

"It *is* business for me. I have a job, you know. You think it's cheap to go to Stanford?"

"I thought you had a scholarship."

"I do. For tuition. Not for room and board. Or books. Or incidentals. I need to make money."

"Where do you work?"

"I work for my neighbors. I babysit their two-year-old on Fridays and Saturdays. They almost always go out."

"Fridays and Saturdays? You're kidding, right? Those are the nights to party."

"This may have escaped your notice, Brett, but I'm not much of a partier. We nerds never are."

He smiled. Then he reached forward and touched my cheek. A tremor raced through me.

"Who said you were a nerd?"

"You did. In sixth grade. And seventh. Remember?"

"Hey. You just accepted my apology for that."

"Right. I can forgive, Brett. I'm just not too quick to forget."

"Wow, I had no idea I hurt you so bad. I really am sorry, Kath. Truly."

He absently rubbed his thumb over my bottom lip. Did

he have any idea what he was doing to me? No guy had ever touched me before.

"You're eighteen, right?" he said.

"Yeah. Last month."

"Me too." He smiled. "I guess we're twins."

I rolled my eyes. "Something like that."

"You want to get a soda or something? To thank you for your help today, you know."

"No, thank you. I have homework to get to."

He was still touching my face. "Come on. A soda'll take fifteen minutes. We don't even have to leave campus. I'll get them out of the machine."

"No."

"Please?"

"Why do want to get me a soda so badly?"

"I don't know." He shrugged his shoulders. "I'm just not quite ready to go home yet."

"Go find one of your jock friends to hang out with. I'm sure they're in the gym doing whatever you guys do."

"What do you think we do in the gym?"

"I don't know. Swat each other with wet towels in the locker room?"

"Hmm. I thought better of you."

"What do you mean?"

"You're stereotyping me. I never did that to you."

"You called me a nerd."

"Correction. *You* called you a nerd. I believe my words were 'who said you were a nerd?'"

I cocked my head. Damned if he wasn't right. Did he really not consider me a nerd?

"I never thought you were a nerd, Kath. And I never thought you were ugly all those years ago. I know I said some mean things. Like I said, I was a stupid punk. I've learned a lot since then. Learned a lot from *you*, actually."

I huffed. "You haven't given me a glance since then."

"That's where you're wrong. I've noticed you a lot. Especially this year. You've grown up, Kath. You've grown into a very beautiful woman."

An anvil dropped to my gut. Eighteen-year-old guys didn't talk like that. He was playing me. I knew it. But why?

"Does Michelle know you go around telling other girls they're beautiful?"

"Michelle doesn't care what I do. She has no say in what I do."

"She's been your girlfriend forever."

"Since tenth grade. Not forever."

"You're getting married."

"Who said that?"

"She did. You forget—I'm on the yearbook and news-paper staff. I know what all the seniors wrote for their plans for the future. She wrote, 'marry Brett and have kids.'"

I shook my head. Such a lofty goal... What could one expect from the head cheerleader who had cotton candy for brains? Michelle Bates was another one of the beautiful people who never lowered herself to talk to me. Not that it mattered much. Michelle was hardly what I wanted in a friend.

Neither was Brett Falcone.

"We might get married," Brett said. "I don't know."

"You didn't hand in a goal sheet for the yearbook," I said. Why I remembered that, who knew?

"No." He cleared his throat. "Not yet."

"It's almost April. We go to print in a few weeks. You better get it in."

"Yeah. I suppose so. Look, about that soda—"

"I can't. But thanks."

"Okay. Next time maybe."

Right. "Maybe. I've got to go. I'll see you here Monday after school."

"Sure you can't do it tomorrow?"

"Positive."

"Okay, then." He shrugged. "Monday it is." He sauntered out of the room and down the hallway.

I gathered my books—and my nerves—and walked down the hallway to Mr. Phillips's office. I peeked my head in, told him the first session had gone well, left the building, and walked the three blocks to my home.

My skin was hot, and then cold. Sweat covered my brow, and my heart thundered.

Damn. Now was not a good time to be coming down with a virus. I inhaled, threw my backpack on the counter, and reached into the refrigerator for a soda. I downed half of it before I realized I was still remembering Brett's touch on my lower lip.

4

Carefully I unfolded the weathered note.

"I've been carrying that around for twenty years," Brett said.

My skin chilled. Sparks settled low in my gut and rushed between my legs as I began to read.

Dear Kath,

I wish I knew where you were, how you're doing. I wish I knew why you left. I thought we had something special. I know it was special to me, at least.

I got the grade I needed in math, thanks to you. I'm going to college in the fall. Michelle and I are getting married tomorrow. She wants to live in an apartment off campus. We're not having a big wedding. Just family at the courthouse. Then we'll find an apartment, and college will start in month.

There's only one problem. I don't want to marry Michelle, Kath. I only want to marry one girl.

But she's gone. I have no way to find her. I've tried every-

thing. I went to your house tonight. I begged your mom to tell me where you are. She wouldn't.

Not a day goes by that I don't think of you, of our time together. I don't regret a second of it, and I hope you don't either. I wish I had told you I love you. I do, you know.

Maybe one day I won't miss you so much. I hope so, because it's too hard.

I wish you the best of everything.

Brett

Tears clouded my vision. "You never said you were in love with me."

"I didn't realize it until you left me."

"I didn't leave you, Brett. We were never officially together."

"I was in love with you, Kath. Desperately in love with you."

"You were eighteen. What did you know about love?"

"I knew what I felt for you was different than what I felt for Michelle."

"Then why did you marry her?"

He shook his head. "Everyone expected it. I wish I had a better explanation. I thought you were lost to me forever. It's always been you, Kath."

Wow. What could I say to that? That I still dreamed of his kisses twenty years later? That being held in his arms had been better than being held in any other man's? That making love for the first time, which should have been the awkward coupling of two virgins, had evoked images and emotion I hadn't seen or felt since?

God knew that was all true. But I couldn't tell him.

There was too much baggage. Too much he didn't know. I folded the note and handed it back to him.

He pushed my hand away. "Keep it. It's yours." He sighed. "You can't tell me you didn't feel anything. You can't tell me our time together meant nothing to you. You're not like that. You were never like that. You wouldn't have done what we did if you hadn't felt something."

True enough. I'd loved him. Loved him like I'd never loved anyone before or since, not even Danny. Hell, especially not Danny. I'd settled. I'd given up trying to recapture what I felt with Brett. I'd wanted a child. Desperately wanted a child. Marriage was necessary, and Danny had been a great candidate—intelligent, a doctor, nice-looking. Who could have asked for more?

I had cared for Danny. It had hurt to break up.

But I hadn't felt the soul-wrenching connection, the oneness, that I'd felt with only one person.

The man sitting across from me now.

"Aren't you going to talk to me?"

I nibbled on my lower lip.

"This is a dream come true, seeing you again. You dropped off the planet, and I thought I'd finally resigned myself to it being over. But you've always been in my mind, Kath. Never far from my heart."

"I don't know what to say to you, Brett."

He reached across the table and took my right hand in his left, rubbed my palm with his thumb.

"Just say you're happy to see me." He smiled.

"Of course I'm happy to see you." I fidgeted, hoping my

hand wasn't too sweaty in his. "I just never expected to hear you say those words."

"I'm sorry. I shouldn't have said it like that. It's the God's honest truth, but I should have gone slower. I'm sorry."

I smiled through trembling lips. "You have nothing to apologize for. You're very sweet, and I loved hearing all of it."

"Good. Glad I didn't scare you away."

"You didn't." He couldn't. "I just never thought I'd see you again."

"You came back."

"Yeah, but I came back to a different suburb from where we grew up. I had no idea you'd be here."

"Fate, I guess." He squeezed the hand he still held. "Luck."

"Maybe. What brought you up here, anyway?"

"Work. I started my own construction company a few years ago, and last year I partnered up with a guy I'd worked under a while back. He had some ideas, and coming up here seemed to work well. Once Michelle and I separated, I didn't need to stay in Edgewood, so here I am."

"Does Zoe live with you full time?"

"Yeah, she does. It worked out better that way. Since I own my own business, my schedule is more flexible than Michelle's. She goes with Michelle on the weekends."

"And your older girls?"

"Candy's nineteen and in her first year of college. Marie lives with Michelle. She wanted to stay at school with her friends."

"Makes sense. Has it been hard on Zoe, being separated from her big sisters?"

"She's acclimated. Kids are great like that."

"Yeah, they are. But Maya really misses Danny. He lives in Cleveland and drives down to pick her up every weekend, but it's hard."

"Divorce is always hard."

"Danny gave me a hard time about moving back here, but I needed to. It's been so long since I've been here. I never came back after I left."

"I know. I looked for you for a while. I eventually gave up."

I shook my head, still fingering the note in my hands. "I can't believe you looked for me."

"Don't get me wrong. I was married to Michelle, and I was always faithful. Even if I'd found you, I still would have been faithful. I just needed to know you were okay. I always wondered."

I swallowed a lump in my throat. All this time, I had been running, trying to make peace with my past. I hadn't given a thought to what my leaving might have done to Brett. "God, Brett, I'm so sorry."

"For what?"

"For leaving you hanging." My eyes misted.

"Hey." He squeezed my hand. "I didn't mean to upset you."

"You didn't. I'm more upset with myself for being so self-centered."

"You were never self-centered, Kath. You always thought of others first."

"Not when I left, I didn't. I... There were reasons I had to leave. Reasons I couldn't tell anyone. I should have thought what it might do to you. I mean... I knew you cared for me. I just had no idea..."

"That I loved you?"

"Yeah. I really didn't. I'm sorry."

"I should have told you."

"Maybe. Maybe I should have told you, too."

"You loved me?"

"In my way, yes, I did." I still did.

"Well, we were from two different worlds. You had a scholarship to Stanford. I was the son of a construction worker. I guess it was never meant to be."

I nodded, and my lips trembled. "Maybe not. But maybe, if things had been different..."

"Things couldn't have been different, Kath, or we wouldn't have been who we were."

Damn. He was right. How did he get to be so intuitive? Then, he always had been. I'd learned so much about him in the short time we'd shared. So much I hadn't expected, so much I hadn't imagined. Brett Falcone was more than a jock, more than the punk kid who liked to make fun of people in middle school. He was intelligent, driven in his own way, highly passionate.

Oh, to be eighteen again.

But I wasn't eighteen. I was thirty-eight. And a mother. A single mother. A single mother who should get my daughter home to bed.

I checked my watch. "It's almost eight. I need to get Maya home."

"Yeah," he agreed. "Zoe needs to get to bed too. Kath, it was great seeing you. Talking to you. I wish…"

"Yeah, me too," I said.

"Can we get together? Talk some more?"

"Maybe over the weekend. Danny picks Maya up at three on Friday."

"Great. I'll drop Zoe at Michelle's around five and then pick you up for dinner. Sound good?"

"Dinner would be wonderful. You need my address?"

"I've got it." He winked. "It's on the soccer paperwork for Maya."

I nodded. "Of course." I called to Maya. "It's time to go, sweetie."

Maya started to complain but then let out an ear-splitting yawn.

"I know a little girl who needs to get to bed."

"I know another one," Brett said.

"It was great seeing you," I said.

"You too." He bent closer and whispered in my ear. "I'll be counting the minutes until Friday."

"Really?" I couldn't help asking.

"Oh, yes," he said. "I'm *positive*."

Positive.

God, he remembered.

Lightning flashed between my legs.

Twenty years earlier

I'D JUST PUT little Terry to bed, and I checked my watch. Seven thirty on a Friday evening and I was babysitting. The story of my life. I hadn't dated, had never been kissed, had never even danced with a guy.

But all that would change in a few months when I went to Stanford. Stanford, where everyone was as smart as I was. Stanford, where no one knew me. No one remembered the awkwardness of my middle school years. To the incoming Stanford class, I'd simply be Kathryn Zurakowsky, the girl with pretty brown hair and eyes, a decent figure, and legs that wouldn't quit. Yes, I'd grown into a pretty woman.

Heck, even the Italian Stallion had said I was a fox. I still couldn't quite wrap my mind around that one.

My tummy growled. I wandered into the kitchen to see what the Rogans had left for me. Debbie was usually good for some decent eats. I peeked into the fridge and found some Black Forest ham and cheddar cheese. A ham sandwich sounded good. Then I spied the leftover pizza box. Mmm, even better.

I pulled out the box and found three pieces of cheesy pepperoni pizza. Perfect. I placed two of them in the microwave, pushed start, and then poured myself a glass of iced tea while I waited.

Ding!

The doorbell. Who would be coming around on a Friday night? Could be the paper boy.

I walked to the door and opened it.

There stood the Italian Stallion himself, complete with math book in hand.

"What are you doing here?"

"You said you were babysitting."

"Yeah. And I am."

"The kid still up?"

"Not that it's any of your business, but no, she's in bed."

"Good. We can study."

"I *am* studying. Government. Not math. I'll see you on Monday after school, Brett."

"Come on. Please? I came all the way over here."

"I'm not allowed to have people over while I babysit." Okay, that was a lie. I often had friends visit while Terry was sleeping. Debbie didn't mind.

"Nice try, Kath. I talked to your mom. She told me where you were and said it would be okay if I stopped by."

Mental note—have a chat with Mom.

"Nobody calls me Kath, by the way."

"Then I'll be the first. I like it."

I kind of liked it too, and that irked me.

"I have my own studying to do."

"It's Friday night. You can study tomorrow."

"Yeah, it's Friday night, so why are you here? Why aren't you out partying with your heavy metal zombie friends?"

He laughed. "Heavy metal zombies? That's rich."

"Whatever. Why aren't you out with your girlfriend?"

"Michelle's out of town for the weekend. Some wedding or something."

"And there's absolutely nothing else for you to do than bother me?"

He smiled, flashing his dimple. "I wanted to see you. I have some questions about math."

"Call me tomorrow, then."

"I'm here now. Come on, please?"

The microwave dinged.

"My pizza."

"You have pizza? Sounds great." He walked through the door.

"Leftover pizza, and it's only two pieces."

"We'll order one then. My treat."

"Brett—"

"Fresh pizza's way better than microwaved leftovers."

I couldn't argue there. "Your treat?"

"Sure." He pulled out his wallet and leafed through it. "I've got a twenty."

"And you want to spend it on pizza?"

"Sure, why not? A guy's got to eat."

What the heck? I'd eat his pizza, help him with his math, and then politely tell him to leave. Deb and Bruce wouldn't be home until well after midnight. Shouldn't be a problem.

"There." I pointed to the phone on the end table. "Call for the pizza. I'll get us something to drink."

I headed to the kitchen and poured another glass of iced tea. "You want sugar in your iced tea?"

"No. Plain's fine."

"Okay." I hastily returned the leftover pizza slices to the fridge.

I walked back into the living room. Brett was sprawled

on the couch looking right at home. Such a beautiful masculine specimen. If only he weren't an asshole.

"All right," I said, sitting next to him. "What seems to be the trouble with your math?"

"Okay, I don't get the whole negative number thing."

"What don't you get about it?"

"How come when you times two negatives together, you get a positive?"

I sighed. I didn't get that either. And for me, someone who needed logic in my life, that didn't sit well. But I'd learned to just accept the rules, apply them, and get the right answer.

"Who cares why that's the case? Just memorize the rule, Brett, and then use it. You'll get the right answer."

"But it doesn't make sense. And then when you times a negative and a positive, you get a negative."

I rolled my eyes. "You know the rules. Just use them. That's all you need to know."

"But I want to understand why."

I wanted to understand too. But I didn't, and it frustrated me. Which was a huge reason why I was *not* majoring in math in college.

"Maybe there is no reason, Brett. Maybe someone just made that up to confuse math students."

"There's got to be a reason."

"God... Okay, do you have any graph paper?"

"Nope."

"We need to make a number line."

"I stopped making number lines in sixth grade, Kath."

"Humor me. Get some notebook paper and draw some vertical lines so we have graph paper."

"Okay." He complied. "Why are we doing this again?"

"Because I don't know the answer to your question."

"You don't?"

"No."

"How can you be so good at math, then?"

"Because I learn the rules. I follow them. I get the right answer. I don't have to understand why."

"Wow. I never would have thought..."

"Well, I never would have thought you'd care about why the rules of math are what they are. I'd have thought you just wanted to get your C and play baseball."

"I do."

"Don't worry. You will, with me tutoring you."

He smiled. "I know."

"You got your graph paper ready?"

"Yup." He handed it to me.

I quickly wrote out a number line starting in the middle with zero and going horizontally and vertically into positive and negative integers.

"Okay. Now, what is your exact question?"

"Well, positive numbers are numbers greater than zero, right?"

"Yeah."

"And negative numbers are less than zero."

"Right."

"When you add two positives together, you get a positive."

"Yup."

"And when you add two negatives you get a negative."

"You got it so far."

"It makes sense so far. When you multiply two positives you get a positive. I don't get why you wouldn't get a negative when you multiply two negatives. I mean, when you think about it, multiplying is just adding, only adding more than once, you know? So if you get negative when you add two negatives, why don't you get negative when you multiply two negatives?"

Wow. Impressive. He'd really thought this out. Determination gripped me. I'd find the answer for him. Clearly, he understood the concepts of addition and multiplication and how they were related. There had to be a reason for this stupid rule. There just had to be.

"Okay, let's look at two times two." I drew a line two blocks to the right horizontally from zero and then two blocks upward vertically from zero. "If we tie these together with coordinates, we get a volume of four on the graph, see?"

"Yeah."

"Now if we do the same with negative two times negative two—" I drew a line two blocks to the left side from zero and then two blocks downward from zero. I shaded in the area. "It's still a volume of four. See?"

"Yeah. But I still don't get it."

I scoffed. "To tell you the truth, neither do I. Did you order the pizza yet?"

"Yeah. While you were getting the drinks."

"Okay, let's think of how multiplication works. Two times two means two sets of two, right?"

"Yeah. And two sets of two would be four."

"Good. And you understand why two times negative two is negative four?"

"Yeah, of course. Two sets of negative two would be negative four. That makes sense."

"Good. It makes sense to me, too. So really, all we need to do is figure out why negative two sets of negative two equals positive four."

"Yup."

"Okay, no problem." I rolled my eyes. "Would you like to know about the existence of God or the meaning of life? That might be easier."

Brett laughed. Oh, he had an attractive, husky laugh. I sighed.

"Do you have any math homework you need help with? Maybe when the pizza comes we can tackle this question. I work better on a full stomach."

Brett laughed again. "Me too. Yeah, here's my home-work assignment. Can you check it for me?"

I went through the problems with him and found he had done a pretty good job. Just as I finished helping him with the corrections, the doorbell rang and the pizza arrived.

"The iced tea's gone, and Deb doesn't have any pop. We should have ordered some Coke," I said.

"No problem. Ice water's fine." He winked. "She does have ice, doesn't she?"

My heart skipped a beat. He'd actually winked at me! "I think so. I'll get us some. And some plates and napkins. Give me a sec."

"I'll be right here."

When I returned Brett had already polished off a piece of pizza.

"You must be hungry," I said.

"Always. Here." He handed me a piece.

I took a bite and set it on a plate.

"So I've been thinking," he said.

"About what?"

"About our positive and negative problem."

"This is really bugging you, isn't it?"

"Yeah. And I have no idea why."

"It bugs me too, and I know exactly why. Because I like to know why. Evidently you do, too."

"I guess so. I never really thought I cared about math. About anything regarding school. I guess I do."

"That's not a bad thing, Brett."

"Maybe not. I *would* like to keep this scholarship. Not that I'm looking forward to four more years of school, but it's better than going to work right now."

"In college, you can find answers to lots more questions."

"I suppose. Of course, Michelle thinks we're getting married. If I go to college, I can put off marrying her."

"Do you *want* to put off marrying her?"

"Yeah. No. I don't know."

"You're only eighteen. It's not a sin to want to put off marriage for a while. I sure don't want to get married right now."

"But you have a future."

"What kind of talk is that? You have a future too."

"I might if I can keep this scholarship."

"You have a future anyway. It's what you make of it that matters."

"I don't want to end up like my dad. Going nowhere in a nowhere job."

"I heard he had an accident. I'm sorry."

"He'll live, but he's on disability for the rest of his life."

"I'm sorry."

"You already said that." He smiled.

"I know. I don't know what else to say. I understand, though, why you want to get your math grade up. You want that scholarship."

"Yeah, I do."

"You've done well. I think you'll be okay. I can continue to meet with you after school."

"But we still need to figure out the answer to our question."

"What question?"

"Why a negative times a negative equals a positive."

"Okay, Brett. But we don't have to figure it out tonight." I took a bite of pizza.

"Why can't we? I'm here. You're here. With my curiosity and your brain, we ought to be able to handle it."

"Okay." I swallowed and took a sip of water. "Let's do some analysis then. We understand why two positives equal a positive, and why a negative and a positive equal a negative."

"Yep."

"So we need to think about why two negatives equal a positive." I inhaled. "I'm stumped."

"I feel a little better if it stumps you, too. You're the smartest person I know."

Heat crept up my neck. He'd said that before. "Am I?" It wasn't like me to be coy, but I couldn't help it.

"Yep, you always have been. I thought for sure you'd know the answer to this."

"Maybe we can figure it out together."

He smiled. "I'd like that." He looked at the graph I'd made. "I wonder..."

"What?"

"Well, you know in English, like a double negative."

Brett Falcone knew what a double negative was? "Yeah. What are you getting at?"

"Like we said, negative two times two is like having two sets of negative two which is negative four, right?"

"So having negative two sets of negative two would be a double negative, right? So that would make it positive."

"Oh my God." I shook my head as a light bulb lit. Had the Italian Stallion truly figured this out? "You're saying that having negative two sets of negative two would be like having two sets of two."

"Yeah. The double negative makes it a positive."

"Oh my God," I said again. "That actually makes sense."

"It does?"

"Yes, Brett, it does!" I jumped up. "If you didn't have two sets of negative two, you'd have two sets of positive two, which would equal the same thing. You're right, it's a double negative! And that explains why it shows a positive volume on the graph."

I picked up the paper and stared at it, awestruck. Brett Falcone was not stupid. Mr. Phillips was right. He was intelligent. He just didn't know it. Very intelligent. And very, very attractive to me right now.

"Amazing. If you had two sets of two, you'd have four. If you lost two sets of two, you'd have negative four. But if you lost two sets of not having two, the double negative results in gaining four. You're a genius, Brett! A genius!"

My heart soared. Knowledge was such a beautiful thing. Emotion swelled within me, and before I could think about what I was doing, I pulled Brett up from the couch and wrapped my arms around him.

And before I knew what was happening, his lips came down on mine.

5

"You haven't changed a bit, Kath," Brett said when I opened the door.

Neither had he. In fact, he looked even better than he had twenty years ago. He was no longer a boy. He was a man. A very handsome, sexy, hot man. My body quivered.

I let out a shaky laugh. "I have a few wrinkles that say otherwise. And the gray hairs."

"I don't see any gray hairs."

"Only my hair stylist knows for sure," I quipped.

"Well, you look beautiful. You were always beautiful."

"Even in middle school?"

He frowned. "I thought we'd gotten past that."

I nodded. What had I been thinking, dredging up that horrible time that we'd gotten past long ago? "I'm sorry. Truly. We got past that twenty years ago. I'm just a little nervous, to be honest."

"Me too." He stepped through the door and shut it behind him. "Let's just get this out of the way then."

He gripped my neck, pulled me into his arms, and lowered his mouth to mine.

His lips—so firm yet so soft at the same time—glided over mine provocatively, grazing at first, barely touching. He traced first my upper and then my lower lip with his tongue. I squirmed. Oh, to be kissed like this again. By Brett Falcone. The one true love of my life. Could it actually be happening?

I would awaken any minute. Slide from the passion of this nocturnal fantasy...

He pressed a sweet kiss to the corner of my mouth and chuckled huskily. "You do remember how to kiss, don't you Kath?"

I couldn't help but smile, remembering our first kiss. My first kiss ever, where he taught me what to do, how to respond.

I'd done a lot of kissing since then, but never with anyone who mattered quite as much as the man in my arms now.

"Kiss me, Kath," he whispered. "Kiss me like you mean it."

Oh, I meant it. Meant it with all my heart. I parted my lips and met his tongue with gentle, silky strokes.

He tasted of peppermint, of maleness, of memory.

Suddenly I couldn't hold him close enough, couldn't kiss him hard enough. As our tongues intertwined, raw guttural moans escaped my throat. I trailed my fingers over his broad, beefy shoulders, his hard chest, plucked open the buttons of his shirt and entwined my fingers in the dark curls covering his pecs. I found a flat nipple, tugged at it, loved how it hardened beneath my fingertips.

And still we kissed, as though we'd never kissed anyone before. He ate at my lips, nibbled, licked, sucked. I returned his passion with equal fervor, drawing his tongue into my mouth and sucking on it. Heat flared between my legs.

God, I was so turned on. More turned on than I'd ever been.

Well, not ever. But not for a very long time.

I wanted him. Wanted him inside me. Wanted to make love with Brett Falcone more than I wanted to breathe.

He broke the kiss and inhaled sharply. "God, Kath." He rained kisses on my cheeks, my nose, the sensitive flesh of my neck.

I shuddered, and my pussy pulsed. I was wet, so wet. So aroused from just a kiss.

But it wasn't just a kiss.

It was a kiss from Brett Falcone. The only man I had ever truly loved.

He sucked at my neck while he cupped my breasts through my blouse. My nipples tightened into aching buds that longed for his lips to suck them, kiss them.

As though he read my mind, he tugged my blouse out of my jeans. The hot flesh of his roving fingers burned. Oh, so good.

"So soft," he whispered. "God, I need to touch you."

"Touch me," I whimpered. "Please."

He reached between my breasts and unsnapped the

front closure to my bra. "Mmm. As full as I remember. Fuller even."

"Having a baby does that," I said, my voice breathless.

"Your nipples are hard, Kath. So hard. God, I want to suck on them."

"No one"—I inhaled a sharp breath—"stopping you that I can see."

"God," he said again. He lifted my blouse over my head and discarded my bra.

I stood, naked from the waist up, as Brett Falcone's dark, smoldering gaze burned into my flesh. And burn it did. I was hot, so very hot.

"Still so beautiful," he said, his voice hoarse. "I always hoped you'd still be as beautiful as the day I first saw you naked, but I never imagined it would be true. You're amazing, Kath."

"Take off your shirt," I said. "I want to see you. Feel you pressed against me. God, Brett. Please."

His shirt quickly met the floor.

"Saints above." I breathed in deeply.

His chest was a work of art. Sculpted perfection. Golden skin covered with a smattering of ebony hair. More hair than I remembered. But of course, he had matured quite a bit since then. Two copper coin nipples poked through, their tips hardened and bronze. I reached for them, traced them, and I reveled in his intake of breath as they hardened even further against my questing fingertips.

I roamed downward, to the bulge in his jeans. I cupped it and squeezed.

"Damn, Kath." He thrust into my hands.

Yes, I'd learned a few tricks since our last time together. Our only time together.

"Are you wet for me?" he asked.

I nodded, still squeezing his hardness through the thick denim. Oh, yes, I was wet. Sopping.

He took my lead and cupped my mound through my jeans, rubbed, found just the right place, and I squirmed. He reached for my zipper.

"I need to feel you. Feel your wetness."

Tingles raced through me and settled in my pussy. Brett slowly unzipped my pants and then reached under my panties until his hot fingers probed my heat.

"Ah, God. So wet, Kath. So wet for me."

"For you," I echoed.

He lowered his head and took a hard nipple between his lips. "So sweet," he murmured.

First, he licked and teased. My nipple hardened until I thought it would burst open. Finally, when I couldn't take it any longer, he closed his lips and sucked on the tight bud.

I squeezed his hardness again, and his groan rumbled against the flesh of my breast. God, I wanted him. Wanted him to stuff that hard cock into me and fuck me hard and fast. Then I wanted to lie in his arms, kiss him and caress him, make slow, sweet, passionate love all night long.

Was this going too fast? Hell, I didn't care. If I had only this—only this one night with him—it would be enough. Two nights with Brett Falcone could get me through the rest of my life.

"I want you," he rasped against my nipple.

"I want you, too."

"Unzip my pants."

I didn't need further urging. I drew the zipper down slowly, listening to each click of the teeth as they brought me closer and closer to my heart's desire. Oh, he was hard. And turned on. A drop of fluid had dampened his boxers. I reached under his waistband and pulled out his thick cock. Then I couldn't wait any longer. I slid out of my sandals, pushed my jeans and panties to the floor, and stepped out of them.

"Condom?" I said.

"Vasectomy."

"Thank God. Take me now, Brett. Don't you dare wait one minute longer."

He wrapped his arms around me, lifted me, and set me down on his hard, thick cock.

Oh, the sweet joining of bodies, of hearts. He slid into me so easily, so smoothly, as though he were made for me.

And he had been. I was sure of it. Surer than anything in the world.

I sighed at that first beautiful fullness, that first smooth thrust that reunited our bodies.

"Brett." My voice had deepened an octave, as though his name had come from the deepest center of me.

My soul.

He lifted me again and brought me back down onto his erection. "God, Kath. It's never been like this with anyone else. Ever."

"For me either."

I slammed my lips onto his and kissed him. Kissed him

with all I had, with all the pent-up frustration of being without him for all those years, with all the love I'd always felt for him and still felt even more acutely now.

Our mouths melded together in a clashing symphony of teeth and lips. No melody, just discordant threads of a chorus too long ignored. Too long silent.

No, the melody would come later. This was fucking. Joining. Hard, fast cementing that we both needed. Later we'd make love.

At least I hoped we would.

I clamped my legs tighter around his waist as he continued to plunge into me. Harder, faster. The room started spinning.

"Brett!" The scream came from my throat yet whirled as though it came from above.

I climaxed with the full force of my desires.

"I feel you coming, Kath. God, I feel you coming." He forced me down onto his hardness with one final thrust, and the contractions of his cock pushed against my wet channel.

"Never like this with anyone else, Kath," he said again. "Never. I swear to you."

$\sim$

Twenty years earlier

HIS LIPS WERE firm against mine. I froze.

Oh, I wanted to kiss Brett Falcone. Wanted it more than my next breath of oxygen, truth be known. But fear paralyzed me. I had never kissed before. What if I did it wrong? What if he laughed at me? I couldn't relive that horrid nightmare of middle school.

He sucked gently against my mouth and then withdrew. "It's okay," he whispered. "Open your mouth. Let me in."

He really wanted to kiss me. Wanted to French kiss me. How sad was it that I was old enough to vote and had never French kissed before?

Well, my days of never having been kissed were about to end. My skin chilled, and fear dashed through me. I took a deep breath through my nose and then parted my lips.

His tongue darted between them. When it touched mine, I quivered. Did I like that sensation?

Yes, I liked it very much.

Tentatively I probed his tongue with mine. A deep moan rumbled from his throat. Did that mean he liked what I was doing? From the moan that echoed from my own throat, I knew the answer was yes.

The surface of his tongue fascinated me. It was silky and wet yet textured, sublime against my own. I swirled mine around it, and then, when a surge of boldness overtook me, I sucked it between my lips and gently bit it.

He groaned louder this time, shoved his tongue farther into my mouth, and kissed me more deeply. My heart thudded. I couldn't catch my breath.

I ripped my mouth away.

"Wow, Kath," Brett said. "No one's ever kissed me like that before."

"Did I do something wrong?"

I hated the words as soon as they'd left my mouth. *That's smart. Just go ahead and tell him you don't have a clue what you're doing.* Of course, he had probably figured that out already.

"God, no. It was amazing." His face came nearer. "Kiss me again."

He took my lips with more force this time, and I parted my own in invitation. His flavor intoxicated me—a little mint, a little tannin from the iced tea, a little spiciness from the pizza. It added up to something I didn't think I could ever get enough of.

When I probed his mouth with my tongue, he sucked my tongue this time. No wonder he had liked that so much! The sensation melted through me like honey— sweet suction, sweet kisses, sweet longing.

The kiss went on and on. Every few minutes he'd break away and suck at my neck, nibble on my earlobe, and then return to my lips and take my breath away once more with drugging kisses.

How long it lasted, I had no idea. I'd have been content to kiss Brett Falcone forever, but when he slid his hand up my side and cupped my breast, I froze.

I ripped my mouth away. "What do you think you're doing?"

"I... I don't know. You seemed to be enjoying the kissing. I just thought—"

"Thought you'd feel me up, did you?"

"Well, yeah. I mean, I'm turned on. You're turned on."

"I... I should never have let this happen. I'm your tutor. It's... It's unprofessional. Unethical."

"You're not my teacher, Kath. You're a student, just like I am. We're both the same age. Both eighteen. We can do whatever we want. And right now I really want to kiss you some more."

So did I. Truth be told, I wanted his hand back on my breast. Fear bolted through me. Not just my breast. I ached for him to touch the throbbing spot between my legs.

"Brett, you have to go now."

"Why?"

"Because Deb and Bruce will be home soon. Or Terry might wake up. And I have my own homework to do."

"It's Friday night, Kath."

Okay, then. "You have a girlfriend, remember?"

He stilled and then plunked down on the couch. "Yeah, I remember."

"What would she think of all this?"

"I wasn't actually thinking about her at the moment."

"That's pretty clear."

"I wanted to kiss you. I like your mouth. It's so pretty. Your lips are pretty, and you have a nice smile. I... I just wanted to feel them against mine. That's all. And when you hugged me—"

"I hugged you because you found the answer to our question. I was impressed, Brett. You're very smart. I never knew that."

"I'm not smart, Kath."

"Yeah. You are. Mr. Phillips told me, and I didn't believe him. But now I do. You have a natural curiosity that shows how intelligent you are. I mean, I've been curious about the whole negatives multiplying into positive thing forever, but I never took the time to sit down and figure it out. To really make a connection between the properties."

"That's what I did?"

I let out a shaky laugh. "Yeah, that's what you did. I'm impressed. But I already told you that."

"You did?"

"Weren't you listening?"

"I actually impressed you?"

"Yeah, you did."

"Wow." His dark eyes softened. "Wow. Here I thought I was the only one who was impressed."

"Impressed by what?"

"By you, Kath. Always you. I've been watching you forever."

I jolted. Had he just said he'd been watching me? "What do you mean?"

"I've watched you grow into one of the most beautiful girls in school."

My skin tingled and my tummy tightened. "Excuse me?"

"You think I don't regret the things I said to you in middle school? I do. I've regretted them ever since. I told you I had no idea how much it hurt you. I knew it was wrong. I let peer pressure control my life. I stopped doing that so much in high school, and I've been a happier person. A better person, I think. Anyway, it's over now. I wish I could take it back, but I can't undo it."

"No, you can't."

"You've always fascinated me. You're incredible. So smart. I always wanted to be smart, to make my parents proud. To be able to do something more with my life than what my parents could. Not that they aren't good parents. But I want more, Kath."

"You can have more."

"Yeah, I think I can. That's why I wanted you for my tutor."

"I thought you wanted me because I was 'a fox.'"

He laughed. "Well, that too. Looking at you is no hardship. But you truly are the smartest person I know." He cleared his throat, and his handsome face reddened. "I've always wanted to know you better. I just didn't know how to approach you, given our past. I didn't know how to apologize to you, to make you understand I never meant any of that. But that's so superficial. I did it. I can't take it back. So I couldn't approach you. Then when this whole baseball scholarship came up and I needed a tutor, I figured this was my chance to spend time with you. Get to know you. Find out if what I was feeling was real."

"What you're feeling? What are you talking about, Brett?"

"I've got a—"

He looked away. Was the Italian Stallion actually embarrassed?

"I like you, Kath. I have for a few years now."

I jerked my head around. "You're playing me."

"I'm not. I swear. I just kissed you, didn't I?"

I longed to believe him, longed for this to somehow be

real, but the image of him and his friends jeering seared into my mind. I swallowed my nausea.

"It's probably some bet with your jock friends. See how long it takes you to get the nerd to fall for you, right? Well, it's not going to happen, Brett. I guarantee it."

"Hey." He stood and gripped my elbow. "I don't kiss anyone I don't want to kiss. You got that?"

"Shouldn't you be kissing your girlfriend?"

He smiled a lazy smile. "She's not here."

"Ha. And I am, is that it? Any port in a storm?"

"No." He raked his fingers through his gorgeous black hair. "You're twisting it all around, damn it."

"Twisting what around? There's nothing to twist around because there's nothing between us. Go back to your buddies and tell them you got the nerd queen to kiss you. Collect your twenty bucks and have a big laugh at my expense."

"Kath, it's not like that. There's no bet. I swear."

"Right. I'm supposed to believe you, the Italian Stallion, wanted to kiss me, Kathryn Zurakowsky, the Pollock, the nerd, the ugly duckling."

"Who's turned into a beautiful swan."

"And what if I hadn't?"

"If you hadn't what?"

"Turned into a beautiful swan? Would you want to kiss me then?"

"I don't know. Would you want to kiss me if I weren't good looking?"

Well, he had me there, and that pissed me off. My blood boiled. "Who said I wanted to kiss you?"

He laughed that time. Damn him.

"For someone who didn't want to kiss me, you gave a good impression of enjoying it."

I *had* enjoyed it. It had been heaven. But I had never kissed before. It would probably be that great with anyone.

"Maybe I'm just a good kisser."

"Ha. Right. If I had a dollar, I'd bet you've never been kissed before."

"Get out." I pulled him to his feet. "Get out. I've had enough of you. You can find yourself another tutor, too. I don't need to deal with you. Go kiss your girlfriend—remember her? Or kiss someone else for all I care. Now get out of here before I call the cops!"

His lips came down on mine again.

6

———

"Wow, Kath." Brett buttoned his pants. "Wow."

I replaced my bra and blouse. "Yeah. I'm sorry."

"God, don't be sorry."

"Oh, I'm not sorry it happened, Brett. I'm sorry I didn't have more self-control. I'm acting like a horny teenager."

"We both were, Kath. We're acting like the horny teenagers we once were. I meant it when I said it's never been like that with anyone else. Not the kisses, not the sex. I mean, I just took you quick and hard against the wall, and I felt more than I've ever felt during the longest love-making session with Michelle."

A spear entered my heart at the mention of Brett's wife. *Ex*-wife. That little prefix made all the difference. He was free to be with me now. And I was free to be with him. Sort of.

He was right about the kisses. An image emerged in my

mind, of Brett and me after our first kiss, and my thought that kissing would be the same with anyone. That the kiss with him had been nothing special.

I'd been wrong. So very wrong.

I'd done a lot of kissing in my life. None had equaled those fumbled attempts I shared with Brett twenty years ago, and none equaled our passionate embraces now.

Still, I'd had unprotected sex. I trusted that he'd had a vasectomy, so I wasn't worried about pregnancy. But I hadn't seen him in twenty years. Who knew who he'd been with? Not the smartest move I'd ever made.

"Uh...Brett?" I fumbled with my hair.

"Your hair looks beautiful," he said, tucking a strand behind my ear. "It's as soft as I remember." He grinned. "What?"

"I don't want to spoil the mood, but...I need to know, you know, that you're clean."

"Clean?"

"Yeah. I know I can't get pregnant, but I don't want to—"

"Kath," he said, looking directly into my eyes. His gaze burned. "I swear to you, I'm clean. I've only been with two women in my life, and you're one of them."

My knees buckled beneath me, and he steadied me.

Truly? The Italian Stallion had never been with another woman?

"I should probably be more concerned about you," he said, "but I'm not."

"Oh?" The insult rankled me. "You don't think I've been with anyone but you and my husband?"

"No, I'm absolutely sure you have."

"Yeah, I have. Plenty, if you want to know." But not a one who had mattered. "So why aren't you more concerned?"

"Because I know you. If there were any issue, you wouldn't have made love to me. You wouldn't have put me in danger."

"True. I'm a doctor."

"Yes, but that's not how I know. I just know *you*. You're a kind, gentle person, and you'd never do anything to harm another living soul."

Especially not one I cared about so deeply.

"No, I wouldn't. But just so you know, I've had all the tests, and I'm clean."

"Well, I had all the tests when I had my vasectomy three years ago, and I'm clean as well. But I didn't need the tests, because I'm serious. I've only been with you and Michelle."

"I can't believe it." I shook my head.

"Why not?"

"Because you're Brett Falcone. The Italian Stallion."

He laughed. "No one's called me that in years."

"You still look the part, I must say. You're still as handsome and delectable as ever."

"And you're still the most beautiful woman I've ever seen. You take my breath away, Kath."

"Wow. *Wow*."

"You keep saying that." He smiled.

"I just can't imagine why you've never been with anyone else."

"I don't know why it's so hard to believe. I married Michelle after you left. She was a virgin on our wedding night. I was married to her until a year ago. I've dated a few women, but there was never enough connection to sleep with them." He pulled me into his arms. "I'd be happy only sleeping with you from now on."

My skin warmed. I could get used this. Get used to being held in his arms, him sniffing my hair, his hands wandering up my back, caressing me.

But too much remained between us that he didn't know about. If he ever found out—

The phone interrupted my thoughts. I pulled away. "I'm sorry. Will you excuse me for a moment?"

"Sure." He kissed my cheek. "Don't be too long, okay?"

My tummy fluttered as I walked to the kitchen and grabbed the phone off the cradle.

"Hello?"

"Yes, hello," a deep masculine voice said. "I'm looking for Kathryn Zurakowsky Abbott."

"You found her. How may I help you?"

"Well," he cleared his throat. "My name is Michael Patton."

"Yes?"

"I...uh..."

"What is it, Mr. Patton?"

"I don't quite know how to say this." He cleared his throat again. "I think I'm your son."

~

Twenty years earlier

I COULDN'T HELP MYSELF. I kissed him back. More than kissed him back. I threaded my fingers through his black hair. It was as soft as I'd imagined. I caressed his muscular shoulders, his biceps, his sinewy forearms. I ran my fingers over the fabric of his shirt, taking in the hardness of his chest, the firmness of his abdomen. I pushed closer to him, snaked my arms around his waist, squeezed the solid globes of his buttocks.

An ache grew in my tummy, my heart. I wanted to touch more of him. His bare skin. To feel his fingers slide over my own bare flesh. My skin heated, my pulse raced, and an inferno blazed between my legs.

He pulled me closer, and his hardness pressed against my abdomen. His penis. I knew what it was. I'd had the sex ed class, the talk with my mother, the gossip with my friends.

I'd never imagined how good it would feel against me, though. How much I'd desire to touch it, to make him feel good...

Out of hand.

This was getting out of hand.

Yet I couldn't break away. Couldn't bring myself to withdraw my lips from the sweet firmness of his, the sweet sensation of his tongue twirling around my own...

Somewhere in the background, the click of a key in a lock.

Deb and Bruce were home!

I pushed Brett away and wiped my mouth. I must look

disheveled. This was not good. They didn't care if I had people over. They'd come home to find me studying with friends before. But this...

I whipped my hands to my lips. They felt tender, swollen. *Oh, my.* Did I look as though I'd just been kissed? Because I sure felt as though I'd just been kissed. Thoroughly, undoubtedly kissed.

I patted down my clothes. Luckily they weren't in disarray. Brett hadn't attempted to feel me again. He looked amazing. Tousled and gorgeous.

"Fix your hair!" I said through clenched teeth.

He shook his head, and it fell into place.

"Now sit down with the math book. Hurry."

I sat down next to him as the door opened.

"Hi, Kathryn," Deb said. "Studying on a Friday night?"

"Tutoring, actually." I tried to sound casual, but my voice shook. I hoped Deb and Bruce didn't notice. "This is Brett. I'm helping him with his algebra."

"Need to get my grades up for baseball," Brett offered.

"Well, then, I see why you're at it on a Friday," Bruce said. "Sports was always my greatest motivation." He pulled his wallet out of his pocket and handed me some bills. "Here you go, Kathryn. Thanks very much."

"No problem. Terry's never any trouble. She's been sleeping soundly since bedtime." I eyed the pizza carton on the coffee table. "Oh, let me just clean up a little."

"No worries," Deb said. "I've got it. You two go on. Enough studying for one night. Maybe you can hit a late show somewhere."

"Oh, I don't think—" I began.

"Yeah, that's a great idea, Kath," Brett said. "How about it?"

"I have studying."

"We've been studying all night."

I bit my swollen bottom lip. We hadn't been studying all night, which was most likely painfully obvious to Deb and Bruce.

"Should I walk you home?" Bruce asked.

"I've got my car. I'll take her home," Brett said.

"Brett, I live right down the street."

"So? Why walk when you can ride with me? Come on."

"Uh...okay. Thanks Deb and Bruce. See you tomorrow afternoon."

"I almost forgot," Deb said. "Our plans fell through for tomorrow, so we don't need you." She winked. "Have a fun evening, Kathryn."

I wanted to expire on the spot. Yes, Deb and Bruce were cool. They probably wouldn't care that I'd been making out with the Italian Stallion in their home. Hell, I'd found a stash of pot in the kitchen cupboards more than once, and Deb routinely left her vibrator out in the bathroom.

Yet embarrassment overtook me. I was *not* Brett Falcone's girlfriend. Would never be. I shouldn't have been kissing him. Still, my body moving without benefit of my mind, I let him guide me out the door, down the driveway, to his Chevy parked on the street. I let him open the door. I slid in, sat on the fabric seat cushion, and inhaled. Pine. A tree-shaped air freshener dangled from the rearview mirror. Nice that he cared how his car smelled. Weird that I cared that he cared.

He got in beside me and started the engine.

"You won't get in trouble for me being there, will you?"

I snapped my mind out of its fog. "No. They don't care."

"Good. I wouldn't want to cost you your babysitting job." He laughed. "Then again, if you lost it, you could spend more time with me."

"With you?"

"Tutoring me, I mean."

"Yeah. I know that's what you meant." But for a moment, a sheer second, I'd hoped he meant he wanted to spend time with me as a person, not as a tutor.

I shook my head to clear it once again. What a fool I was.

"This is where I live," I said.

"I know where you live."

"You do?"

"An address isn't that hard to find, Kath."

"Why do you call me Kath? No one does."

"So you said." He cocked his head. "It fits you. How come everyone calls you Kathryn?"

"My mom calls me Kathy."

"But no one else?"

"No. I prefer Kathryn."

"You want me to call you Kathryn?"

No! For some reason I couldn't quite figure out, I wanted him to call me Kath and nothing else.

I shook my head again. Damn spider webs were invading my brain.

He parked the car in the street by my house. Without

looking at him, I opened the door and left the car. I turned back, polite to a tee. "Thanks for the ride."

"No problem. I'll walk you up."

"No. Please don't. This isn't a date."

"I didn't say it was, but I want to walk you up."

Something in his voice made me relent. He walked me to the front porch and stood with me under the door.

"Thanks for helping me out tonight," he said.

Could he tell my body had turned to jelly? My legs quivered. "You're welcome. I'll see you after school Monday in the usual classroom."

"How about tomorrow?"

"I have my own homework to do tomorrow."

"You might need a break. We could get ice cream or something."

Okay, this was so not happening. Brett Falcone was not asking me out on a date. Especially not Brett Falcone who was going out with Michelle Bates.

Damned if I didn't want to have ice cream with him.

"Okay. Pick me up at three. I'll have my work done by then."

"You got it." His smile lit up his face. He bent near me and brushed his lips lightly across mine.

I jolted, and a fire ignited between my legs. Just a little peck and, oh God, I wanted more.

"Good night, Kath."

"Good night."

I floated inside.

7
———

The phone clattered on the ceramic tile kitchen floor.

"Kath?" Brett's voice haunted me from the other room. "You all right in there?"

Brett! What timing this Michael had. But I had to speak to him. Had to find out if he was truly the little boy I'd given away all those years ago.

I willed my throat to relax, my voice to steady. "I'm fine. I have to take this call. I'll just be a minute."

My shaky hand retrieved the phone.

"I'm sorry," I said into the mouthpiece. "You took me by surprise."

I walked from the kitchen past Brett, waving at him and mouthing "a patient," stumbled into my bedroom, and shut the door behind me.

"All right, Mr. Patton."

"Call me Michael."

"Of course. Call me Kathryn."

"I got your name from the agency. The records said that once I was eighteen, if I wanted to contact you, I could. I did a little research and found your married name. It was just a stroke of luck that you're still living in the same city."

"When's your birthday?"

"January fourth."

Right date. *Holy shit.* "All right." My stomach burned. My son. My beautiful, precious son.

Brett's son.

Lord, now I'd have to tell Brett.

If I wanted to start a relationship with him, I had to tell him anyway. A relationship built on a lie was no relationship at all. I'd hoped for a little more time. A little more time to get used to the idea, to get *him* used to the idea...

"I know this is coming out of nowhere for you," Michael said, "but I really do want to meet you. And I have a question to ask you."

"What?"

"Well, the adoption papers don't specify who my father was."

"No." I hadn't written it down. Hadn't wanted Brett to ever know. Had wanted him to play baseball, to have the life he deserved.

"You...*do* know who he was, right?"

"Yes. He was...*is*...a fine man."

"Oh, good. I just didn't want to be the product of a rape or anything."

"Oh, no. Nothing like that. I loved your father. I was just young, and he was...engaged to someone else."

"Oh. I see."

"I wish I could have kept you. I do, Michael. But I was eighteen, and I had a scholarship."

"It's okay. My mom and dad are great, and I have two sisters."

"You have another sister. Maya, my daughter, is four."

"Oh?"

"And...three other sisters. Your father... He has three daughters."

"So you still keep in contact with him?"

"I...recently renewed contact, yes."

"I don't want to push you, but can we meet? I've just always wondered what you look like. Where my nose comes from, things like that."

"I suppose." My nerves skittered.

"And my father? Could I meet him?"

"Oh, God." I sighed. "Michael..."

"He doesn't know about me, does he?"

"No. I'm so sorry. He just came back into my life."

"Aren't you going to tell him?"

"Yes. I just need to find the right time."

"I understand. Until you find the right time, maybe you and I can meet."

I smiled into the phone. "I'd like that. I truly would. You probably won't believe this, but I've missed you all these years. A day has not gone by that I haven't thought of you. I always hoped I'd made the right decision."

"You did. I have a great life."

Relief swept through me. "You have no idea how glad I am to hear that." I grabbed a pad of paper from my bureau.

"I wish I could talk longer, but I need to go. I have company. Could you give me your number? I'll call you."

"Okay."

I hastily scribbled down the name and number on the pad. "I'm so glad to hear from you, Michael. You have no idea."

"Good. I'm glad I didn't disrupt your life."

"Oh, no. You couldn't. I'm so happy you've had a good life, and I do want to know you. I'll call you. Or you can call me anytime, okay?"

"Thank you...Kathryn. I appreciate it."

"Bye now."

"Bye."

I drew in a deep breath. *Brett.*

Brett was in the other room and had no idea he had a son.

I'd never told him. Had I made the wrong decision? Would he understand my reasoning? Or would he be angry?

Oh, God, he'd be angry...

I wanted to be with him. Wanted to make love with him again. Wanted all the passion and excitement I'd given up twenty years ago. The passion and excitement I'd never felt with another man in all this time.

We still had a dinner date. Maybe I could tell him in a public place, where he wouldn't have a fit...

What if he hated me? I couldn't bear the thought. What if he walked away? Forever? When I'd just found him again?

I clutched the phone in my hand as my eyes misted. I walked numbly out of the bedroom.

"You okay?" Brett came toward me. "You look a little off."

I sniffled. "A patient. He's okay though. It's just hard sometimes."

"I bet it is. You're such a caring person. You must hurt when they hurt."

If he only knew. "Yes. It's difficult. A doctor is supposed to keep a professional distance."

"How can you? They're people. People you get to know."

"Yes, they are." I smiled. "You get it."

"Of course, I get it. I get *you*, Kath. I always have."

Yes, he always had.

"Ready for dinner?"

I nodded and grabbed my jacket. We drove, holding hands and not talking, to a small Italian place that someone in the Falcone family owned. I joked with Brett about being related to half of Columbus. Seemed like all the central Ohio Italians were bound by blood in one way or another. But the Falcones were never a mafia family, Brett maintained, despite the rumors.

I remembered those rumors. Those rumors that had nearly cost Brett his life. And me mine.

$\sim$

Twenty years earlier

I HADN'T LAUGHED SO MUCH in ages. Turned out we both loved chocolate—the richer, thicker, and darker the better.

I followed Brett outside the door of the ice cream shop.

He turned and drew me near, and I gasped as he brushed his lips and tongue over the corner of my lips.

"A little chocolate," he said, smiling.

Anyone could have seen us. The ice cream shop was a popular hangout. No one from school had been there today, true, but still. I couldn't believe he'd done such a thing.

What would Michelle think?

Well, if Brett didn't care what Michelle thought, why should I? I wouldn't go out of my way to kiss him, but if he kissed me? Why fight it?

I wanted to kiss him. Had never imagined such an intimate feeling as his lips on mine. Couldn't wait to start kissing him more. To kiss other men more. I'd be the kissing queen!

"Let's walk behind the mall, in the alley," Brett said.

"Why?"

"So I can hold your hand, kiss you."

"Why do you want to hold my hand and kiss me?" I had to know.

"Because I want to. It feels nice. Doesn't it feel nice to you?"

"But Michelle—"

"Michelle's not here."

"You're not breaking up with her, are you?"

"I haven't really thought about it. We're not married. I'm not being unfaithful."

"I think you are. I think you and she have an understanding."

"Maybe *she* has an understanding. I don't."

"She thinks she's marrying you, remember?"

"I might. I might not. Right now, I don't want to think about Michelle. I want to walk with you in the alley. I want to hold your hand. I want to put my arms around you and kiss you."

"Wow." The word came out in a breathy rasp. The Italian Stallion a romantic?

He took my hand and tugged me along. "Come on."

We walked behind the mini mall into the back alley that was deserted and a little scary. But no fear seized me. Brett was big and strong and would protect me.

He held my hand, and then, when I least expected it, pushed me against the back of a store building and crushed his mouth to mine.

My lips tingled, and my heart raced. The kiss consumed me, became me. Nothing existed in the world except Brett and me and the mating of our mouths.

Until—

I jerked when the stark chill of a blade slid against the warm flesh of my neck.

"Nice piece of ass, Falcone. Care to share?"

The voice slithered over me like snake venom. Two muscled thugs pulled Brett from me while the third pressed the cool steel into my flesh. My heart stampeded as fear pulsed into me.

"What the hell do you guys want?" Brett demanded.

"The same as always, Falcone. You know what we're after."

"And I've told you before. You've got the wrong Falcone. I'm Julian Falcone's son. You're looking for Angelo Falcone's son. No relation."

"Bullshit."

"No lie."

He glanced at me. I swallowed audibly.

"At least let *her* go."

"Not a chance."

"She's a Zurakowsky. No relation to the Family, honest."

I closed my eyes and prayed. What a time for him to bring up my Polish name. But if it worked, so help me, I'd give thanks the rest of my days for being the brunt of Pollock jokes.

"We have a message for your old man," the man holding the knife to me said.

"His old man is home in bed," I said, shaking. "He's a construction worker, for God's sake. A construction worker on disability."

One of them punched Brett in the stomach. He doubled over with an *oof*.

I cringed but held still, ever aware of the blade still scraping against my neck.

"Let her go, man," Brett huffed. "Please."

"I'm not going anywhere without you," I said through clenched teeth.

"It's not worth it, Kath." His voice was raspy, breathless.

"I'm not leaving you!" The exclamation stretched my vocal cords and the blade pressed farther into my skin.

"You harm a hair on her head and I'll see all of you dead," Brett seethed.

My heart pounded, and my stomach churned. Yet a little bit of joy surged through me at Brett's protection.

"You give your old man our message, Falcone."

"Fine. I'll give it to him. But I swear to God you've got the wrong man."

"Give him this." The thug to Brett's right clocked him in the jaw. Not a pop, like I'd heard in movies. The punch hit Brett's face with a dull thud.

The thud rang in my head.

"Next time, we hurt the girl," he said.

The two let Brett go and he fell into a heap. The other pressed the blade into my flesh once more, removed it, and fled. I rushed to Brett and knelt beside him.

"My God. Are you all right?"

"I'll live," he said breathlessly.

"Can you get up? Come on, I'll help you."

"I'm fine. This isn't the first time those bozos have mistaken me for the wrong Falcone."

"What can you expect from morons?" I helped him stand. "Come on. We'll go to my house and get you cleaned up. My parents are out for the day and won't be home until after ten."

"You don't have to, Kath." Then he turned, his eyes wide. "Are you okay?" He reached toward me, trailed one finger along the burning flesh of my neck. "If they hurt you, so help me, I'll—"

"Do what? Take down three giants yourself? I don't think so. I'm fine. They didn't hurt me. *You're* hurt. And I'm going to take care of you. Come on."

8

"Did you ever regret not having a son?" I asked Brett as I tore another piece of Italian bread from the loaf.

"Only a little," he said. "I mean, sure, part of me always wanted a chip off the old block." He smiled. "But I love my girls. They're everything to me."

Yet his voice held a whisper of regret.

"But still..." I urged.

"Yeah, I would have liked to have a son."

You have a son. His name is Michael, and he wants to meet us.

My heart thumped. How could I tell him without him hating me for keeping it from him?

"How about you? Did you want a boy?"

"I was thirty-four when I had Maya. I was pretty sure she'd be my one and only. I didn't care whether she was male or female, as long as she was healthy."

"She's a beautiful little girl, Kath. She looks just like you."

"Thank you." The warmth of a blush raged up my neck. "She does favor me, though she has Danny's eyes. He has those gorgeous icy blue eyes. I'm glad Maya got them. They're so noticeable."

"I like your warm brown ones, Kath," Brett said, smiling. "Though Maya is beautiful. I don't mean to say she's not."

"I know." I smiled. "Tell me. Do your other girls look like Zoe? In other words, like mini Bretts?"

He laughed. "Candy does. Marie favors Michelle more. Still dark hair and eyes, like me, but her facial features are softer, a little curvier, like Michelle."

"I'd love to meet them."

"Okay. We'll plan on it sometime. Does that mean..."

"Mean what?"

"That you want to...be with me? I mean, I hope you do. It's what I want. It's all I've ever wanted, to be honest."

My insides melted and I nodded. "But we don't know each other very well, Brett. We never did, really."

"We knew each other in the biblical sense." He smirked.

I couldn't help but return his roguish grin. "Evidently, we still do. But really. It's been twenty years. There's so much about each other we don't know. That we need to learn."

"We'll have fun learning." He reached across the table and took my hand, massaging my palm gently with his thumb. "I want to know everything about you, Kath. Every single thing. I want to know what kind of dressing you like on your salad. What you like to watch on TV. What kind of books you like to read. What makes you laugh, smile, cry. Everything."

"That's lovely." My eyes misted. There was so much he didn't know. So much he needed to know. I opened my mouth to tell him but lost my nerve.

"I mean it. Every word. I shouldn't have married Michelle when I loved you. I should have chased you down. Found you. Convinced you I could give you what you needed."

I shook my head. "We were different people then, with different needs. You deserved the chance to play baseball."

"I know. I guess I couldn't compete with Stanford."

"Oh, it wasn't just that." *God no, it wasn't just that. If he only knew...* "You and Michelle had a history. And you had a baseball scholarship."

"That only lasted a year."

"I know. I'm sorry you had to quit school and work."

"It wasn't just that." He looked down.

"What is it?"

"I injured my knee. Had a few surgeries. I'm fine. I mean, I get around fine, no limp. But it ended my baseball career."

"Oh, Brett, I'm so sorry."

My heart sank. All this time I felt I'd done the right thing, keeping our child a secret. I wanted him to have the chance to play baseball. I wanted him to have the chances for so many things—the chances he deserved. Now, to find out baseball never would have been possible... Shivers raced up my spine. Had I made the wrong decision? Would he have wanted the baby? Would he have wanted *me?*

"It's okay. I enjoyed school, but I never would have done as well without you there to help me."

I smiled and shook my head. "You never needed me, Brett. I shouldn't tell you this, but Mr. Phillips, the counselor, remember him? He confided in me when he was trying to get me to tutor you that you had scored in the superior range on the state tests."

"Superior? What's that mean exactly?"

"It's one ranking below genius level."

"I suppose you scored at the genius level?"

"Yes, but just barely. There isn't that much difference between where you and I scored."

"Really?" Happiness glowed on his face. His brows lifted. "I wonder why no one ever told me."

"*I* told you. I told you how smart you were."

"Yeah. But I thought you were just being nice. You know, being a good tutor."

"I'm not that nice a person."

"Sure you are. You were always nice. I remember that day you took care of me when those guys attacked me. I don't think anyone's ever taken such great care of me since."

I shuddered.

That day.

That fateful day that had led to our son.

∽

Twenty years earlier

BRETT JERKED as I touched the warm washcloth to his cheek.

"I'm sorry. I have to clean it before I can help you."

We sat together on the sofa in my living room.

"It's okay. Just stings a little."

"I know. Again, I'm sorry."

"I'm sorry, Kath. I'm sorry you had to witness that. Sorry you had to be in the middle of it. All I wanted to do was protect you."

"You did."

"Hell, no, I didn't."

"Well, you couldn't do much when there were two gorillas holding you, could you? It doesn't matter. We're both okay and out of danger."

"You shouldn't have had to see that."

"So they got the wrong guy. I know there's mob around here. Everyone knows, Brett."

"At least you don't have a mob name."

"Nope. I've got a Pollock name."

Brett reddened. "I'm sorry."

"Sorry that I'm Polish? I'm not."

"No. Geez. I mean sorry I used to call you a Pollock."

"Everyone did. Polish jokes were the rage, remember?"

"Yeah, I know. Better a Zurakowsky than a Falcone. The mob'll never mistake *you* for someone they're after."

I couldn't help but chuckle. "I actually had that same thought today, during the whole thing. Never have I been so thankful for my Polish roots."

He laughed with me. "Ow, that hurts!"

"Then stop laughing." I smiled as I cleansed the rest of the dried blood from his cheek. "Now I just need some anti-bacterial ointment or something. There isn't much blood. But you're going to swell up, I bet."

"Won't be the first time."

"You mean they've come after you before?"

"Not those three, but others. It's never the same ones twice. They find out they made a mistake, and then they leave me alone."

"Who are they after?"

"Brad Falcone. He's a junior at Bishop Academy. His dad is an attorney with lots of mob ties."

"Oh." I didn't know what to say to that, so I made small talk. "I guess Brad sounds a lot like Brett."

"Especially when you have the IQ of a tomato."

I laughed. "See, you *are* intelligent. You can recognize when someone is stupid."

"I don't need to be intelligent to recognize a moron, Kath."

"I suppose not. But you *are* smart. I'm still amazed that you figured out the whole negative times negative equals positive thing."

"Are you *positive*?"

"Yeah. *Positive*."

Stupid joke between us, but it made me warm. Brett and I had a private joke.

Silly, but nice. Nice and warm and fuzzy.

Geez, Kathryn, you're getting all fluffy and perfumey, like Michelle Bates. Can't have that. I was not the frou-frou cheerleader type that Brett Falcone liked. I never would be.

Yet he seemed to like me. He liked kissing me, and he was leaning toward me now.

"Just a minute." I backed away. "I'm not done with you yet." I squeezed some anti-bacterial ointment onto my fingers and rubbed it gently over his cheek.

He winced.

"I'm sorry. I'm trying not to hurt you."

"I know."

When I finished, I went to the kitchen, scooped Belgian chocolate ice cream into two bowls, returned, and gave one to Brett.

"Here. You look hungry."

He laughed. "Shit, that hurt. I am, actually." He took a bite of ice cream and winced. "Hurts to open my mouth, though."

"I know. I'm sorry." I scooped some ice cream into my spoon, but on its way to my mouth, the cold custard glopped onto my neck. *Nice. Be a clutz in front of the Italian Stallion.* Could this day get any better?

Before I could grab a tissue from the box on the end table, Brett leaned forward and licked the ice cream off my warm skin. Tingles shot through me. Without thinking, I wrapped my arms around his neck and brought his mouth to mine.

Chocolate dreams... His tongue found mine and danced around it. His mouth hurt, I knew, but it didn't seem to faze him. The kiss was raw and pure. Raw emotion and pure need. Pure love.

At eighteen, could I really be in love? With the Italian Stallion?

When he trailed kisses down my neck, licking up the last of the ice cream, I closed my eyes and sighed.

Yes, I love him. I loved Brett Falcone.

My hand shaking, I reached toward the crotch of his jeans and touched the bulge underneath. It pulsed against my fingers.

He moaned. "Kath, are you sure?"

Was I?

A little over an hour earlier, a knife was pressed to my flesh. My life could have ended, and what would I have had to show for it?

For once, I wanted to live in the moment. Take what I wanted and think nothing of the consequences.

"Yes, Brett," I said, my voice a raspy sigh, "I'm sure."

9

Nerves. Tingling nerves. I swallowed as I closed the door behind Brett.

He turned to me and smiled. "I love you, Kath." He cupped my cheeks. "I want you."

How easy it would be to surrender to him again, to let the lust take me away from what I faced.

But no. I shook my head. "We need to talk first."

"Really?" His lips turned slightly downward. "We talked a lot at the restaurant. I want to be with you. Isn't that what you want?"

God, yes, it's what I want, what I've always wanted.

But I had to clear the air before I succumbed again. He deserved that much.

"I do want you, Brett. I want to be with you in every way I can, but"—I choked back a sob—"there's something I have to tell you."

"What, baby?" He caressed my cheeks with his thumbs. "What is it?"

"Let's sit." I led him to the living room, sat down on the couch, and patted the seat next to me.

He sat, his handsome face racked with concern. "Kath?"

I swallowed again. "Please don't hate me."

He touched my arm gently. "I could never hate you. Believe me, I tried. I wanted to hate you when you disappeared. I couldn't."

Oh, God. Queasiness seized my tummy. He had wanted to hate me for leaving, and he didn't know why I left. When he found out...

Could I put it off? Have one more night of passion with him before facing the piper?

No. I braced myself and steadied my emotions. He had to be told.

"I loved you then, Brett, and I love you now. I wouldn't have given you my virginity if I hadn't—" A sob caught in my throat. I cleared it.

"I know that now." His deep voice soothed me. "It's okay."

"But it's not okay. I'm afraid it will never be okay, what I did."

"Just tell me, Kath. I love you. That won't change."

I didn't doubt he thought he spoke the truth. But he had no idea what was coming.

"I left town for a reason, and I started college late for a reason. The reason is... His name is Michael. He's my son."

Brett's eyes widened. "What? You were pregnant?"

I nodded. "*Our* son, Brett."

Brett sat, immobile except for a slight tremble in his full lips.

"I love you. Please say something."

Several minutes passed. I fidgeted, afraid to touch the man I loved.

"Please, Brett."

"Michael. You know him?"

I shook my head. "He just found me. I haven't met him yet."

His features softened for a moment. Did he understand? Would everything be all right?

My hopes dashed when he came to life, his dark eyes blazing.

"Don't you think I deserved to know?" His handsome face reddened. "Or did you think at *all*?"

I gulped. "Of course I thought. All I *did* was think."

The anguish so long buried slammed back into me as though it were yesterday. The yearning for a child I'd never know by a man no one knew I loved. The stigma of being the girl in trouble. Not just the girl in trouble, the class valedictorian in trouble. The heartache, the loss, the absolute fear.

"You deserved a chance to play baseball. God knows you earned it. I had no idea you were going to run and marry Michelle."

"I wanted you, Kath. *You*. We could have made a life together with our child."

"What kind of a life? You had a scholarship to Ohio State, and I had one to Stanford. That's a heck of a commute, Brett."

"I would have given up baseball."

I shook my head. "That's not what I wanted."

"What *you* wanted?" He paced, rage staining his face. "Did you give a thought to what *I* might want?"

"A child? A child at eighteen? Who would want *that*?"

"I had one the next year, anyway. What would it have mattered?"

I balled my hands into fists. "Maybe it's not what *I* wanted. Did that occur to you? Maybe I wanted to go to Stanford and then to medical school. That was always my dream. Do you have any idea how hard med school is on married people? Over half the ones I knew ended up divorced. Would you have wanted *that*?"

The sadness in his beautiful dark eyes haunted me.

"You didn't want our child?"

Nausea gripped my insides. "That's not what I meant, Brett. Of *course* I wanted our child. I *still* want our child. But I knew another family could give him more than either you or I could at that time."

"Damn it, Kath." His fist came down on my coffee table. "I never imagined you could betray me like that. Whether you were right or wrong, I had a right to be involved in the decision."

I said nothing. What *could* I say? He was right.

My head fell into my hands as he walked silently out of my living room, out of my home.

Out of my life.

Twenty years earlier

I WASN'T nervous as Brett peeled my clothes from my body.

I wasn't nervous as he then undressed himself.

I wasn't nervous when he took my hand in his and led it to the private part of him between his legs.

If ever anything felt completely right in my life, this did.

This.

I stood, naked, wrapped in Brett's arms, our lips fused together and our tongues dueling.

I throbbed between my legs, even more so when Brett trailed one hand downward to my private place.

His dick pulsed against me, and he broke the kiss. "Kath, you're so wet. You're ready for me."

I couldn't speak, so I merely nodded.

This wasn't happening. Couldn't be happening.

Yet it was.

I was going to lose my virginity to Brett Falcone.

The Italian Stallion.

Only he was no longer the Italian Stallion.

He was Brett. Simply Brett. And he was nothing like I'd thought.

Brett was intelligent. Brett was caring. Brett was kind and gentle. Brett was funny and made me laugh.

And Brett wanted to make love to me. To Kathryn Zurakowsky.

He rained tiny kisses over my jawline and down my shoulder to my breast. My nipples were hard and taut, begging for his attention.

"You're so beautiful," he said.

Warmth surged through me. Warmth, and a feeling so pure I knew instinctively what it was.

Love.

When Brett flicked a finger over one nipple, I wasn't sure I'd ever felt such intense pleasure. Until he took it between his lips and sucked.

I lost all thought, then, and only feeling remained. Raw, intense feeling that whirled through me and around me, almost visible as it encased us in a cloud of love.

I *loved* Brett Falcone.

He didn't love me back. He belonged to another. But I loved him, and I chose to give him this gift I could give only once.

And I imagined that he loved me too.

I gave in to the emotion, and when he entered me, I welcomed the sharp stab.

"Okay?" he asked.

"Yes, keep going. Please."

With each thrust the pain lessened, and soon only pleasure remained. Pleasure, and a sense of completeness I'd never known, and that I was sure I'd never know again.

That didn't matter. If I had only this moment with Brett for the rest of my life, it would be enough.

This stolen afternoon of passion could hold me forever.

10

I sat in my car and fingered the delicate note Brett had given me two weeks earlier. A tear fell onto the discolored paper. What had I expected? That he'd understand? I'd kept a child from the man I loved.

He'd walked out without kissing me, without making plans to see me again. I'd enlisted the babysitter to take Maya to soccer practice in the days following. I couldn't face him. Not yet. I'd eventually tell him how to get in touch with Michael, and perhaps we could regain a friendship. But I had no doubt lost him as a lover, as a soul mate. That I'd betrayed him pierced my heart like a poisoned dagger.

I placed a gentle kiss on the note before folding it and placing it back in my purse.

I cleared my throat, choking away more tears, and turned the ignition.

"Oh!"

The rap on the windshield startled me.

Brett.

I wiped my eyes and rolled down the window.

His beautiful eyes were sunken and sad. "Hi, Kath."

I sniffled. "Hi."

"Can we talk?"

"I'm on my way out, as you can see. Maybe later?"

"Please?" He walked around the car, opened the passenger door, and sat down.

"I'm on my way to meet someone."

Our son. I'm on my way to meet our son.

"Can it wait a few minutes?"

I shook my head.

No, it can't wait. I'm already twenty years late.

"What do you want, Brett?"

He tentatively touched my hand. Sparks slid over my flesh. Always sparks, always with Brett. Never with anyone else.

"I want to apologize."

My heart jolted. "Apologize? You have nothing to apologize for. This was all me."

His full lips trembled and he shook his head. "I was only thinking about myself. I didn't think for a minute about what you went through. I wish I had been there for you. I wish you had told me."

I gulped and nodded. "I wish I had, too. I did what I thought was best at the time for both of us. But I was wrong. You had a right to be involved in the decision, whether or not you loved me. I didn't know you did."

"I know. I should have told you."

"It's okay. We both made mistakes."

He squeezed my hand. "And we'll probably make more. One thing I know though. You're the one I want to be with when I make them, if you'll have me."

Tears welled in my eyes. He still wanted me?

"I've waited twenty years for you, Kath. I don't want to wait any longer." He caught a tear on my cheek with his index finger.

"Oh, Brett." I sniffed back my tears, my heart soaring toward the moon. I leaned toward him and brushed my lips over his. "Buckle up, then."

He complied. "Where are we going?"

I smiled. "To meet our son."

THE END

Sign up for my newsletter here:
http://www.helenhardt.com/signup

Find more vintage collection here!

Read on for an excerpt from *Rebel*!

REBEL

WOLFES OF MANHATTAN ONE

When Rock Wolfe was fourteen, he tried to kill his father.

Twenty years later, someone else finished the job.

Now Rock is returning to New York for the reading of the billionaire's will. No way did Derek Wolfe leave anything to his oldest son, but according to Rock's brother, his presence is required.

Estate attorney Lacey Ward isn't looking forward to the reading. None of Derek Wolfe's children will be happy, least of all his oldest. When Rock enters the conference room, Lacey is stunned. He's a rebel—a biker all muscled and gorgeous in black leather. This won't be easy, especially since she can't stop staring at him.

Rock pays no attention to the reading. He's lost in a fantasy of bending his father's hot attorney over a desk. He's not a commitment kind of guy, though, and she screams white picket fence. Sparks fly between them, but the murder lurks in the back of their minds.

Rock knows all his family's secrets...or so he thinks. Mysteries seem to hide everywhere—mysteries that threaten not only his and Lacey's future but their lives as well.

EXCERPT:

When I was fourteen years old, I tried to kill my father.

The stunt had cost me my freedom. I'd have gladly spent the rest of my life imprisoned as the love slave of a Greek battalion had I been successful. But to be put through hell when the bastard was still alive? So not worth it.

Military school. Not just any military school, but a private academy where millionaires sent their troubled kids to be beaten down, where the rules were that there were no rules. Where survival of the fittest was no longer reserved for the animal kingdom.

I survived.

I grew stronger living through the hell that was Buffington Academy. Secluded in the Adirondacks, the school was home to the most spoiled young men in the world... and the most troubled. After two weeks, I knew I didn't belong there, but I spent four years in that hellhole.

Those years made me wish for juvie.

But no, my parents didn't turn me in. Instead...Buffington.

I spent those years plotting my father's demise, but of course by the time I turned eighteen and released myself, I knew better. I'd learned my lesson. My father wasn't worth it. Trying to take him out had cost me four years of my life.

Even so, I dreamed of his death. It was no less than he deserved.

But when it finally happened, I was totally unprepared.

"Dad's dead," my brother Reid said into the phone when I answered.

I froze, as if ice water had replaced the blood in my veins.

"Did you hear me?"

"Yeah. Yeah. What happened?"

"We're not sure yet. But I have to ask you, bro..."

"What?"

"Were you anywhere near Dad's penthouse last night?"

"Are you fucking kidding me?"

"Someone shot him in the head in the penthouse."

I couldn't help a chuckle. Most guys might freak out hearing this kind of news. Not me. The bastard had it coming.

"They're going to get in touch with you," Reid continued.

"I'm at my cabin, Reid. And by the way, you don't sound too broken up."

"None of us are. He was a bastard. That's public knowledge."

"So why the interrogation? There're a thousand people who probably wanted him dead."

"True, but Dad sent you away when you were so young. The cops are going to think you might be getting back at him."

"Don't you think I'd have done something before now?"

"Whatever, man. Still, Riley, Roy, and I need to know. Did this in any way involve you?"

"I just told you. I'm home."

"You could have hired it out."

Seriously? I'd been a model citizen since I left Buffington—well, maybe not model in the sense of perfect, since I'd been arrested in a biker brawl once, but I hadn't started it and the charges were dropped. I'd driven after too many drinks a few times, but I hadn't gotten caught. I'd made my own money, never stole a dime. And never took one penny from that motherfucker who'd fathered me. Not that he would have given me any. I had a few biker buds who might have been able to handle a contract on a human life, but I'd have never asked.

The asshole warranted better than a paid hitman who bore him no ill will. He deserved to be taken out by someone he'd wronged, someone who could look into his cold eyes so he knew who was doing the deed.

There were a ton of us out there.

"I didn't," I told my brother. "Trust me. I had nothing to do with it. But I'm glad the asshole's dead."

"None of us are crying, like I said." Reid sighed through the phone line. "Thank God."

"Relieved, are you?"

"Of course. You're my big brother. I don't want you rotting in prison for the rest of your life."

I hadn't seen my brothers and sister in years. Reid was the only one who kept in touch with me regularly. I heard from Roy and Riley every once in a while. Roy didn't keep in touch with anyone, and Riley had her own issues.

"I won't be. I was out on a ride last night with buddies who can vouch for me. I got in around one a.m."

"They think the murder occurred around four this morning. You couldn't have gotten here by then."

"Plus the fact that I'm still in Montana right now."

"Yeah. Right. I'm not thinking straight." Reid cleared his throat. "You need to get on the next flight to New York."

"Fuck that. I'm not coming home."

"You have to. The cops want to talk to you."

"There's this little thing called a phone."

"Damn it, Rock. You need to come home."

"Burn him and be done with it. You don't need me for that."

"We haven't made any funeral arrangements yet."

"What do you need me for, then?

"The attorneys are reading Dad's will tomorrow morning."

"Why the hell should I care? You know he didn't leave me a damned penny."

"It specifies that we all have to be present. They won't read it without you there."

"You've got to be kidding me." The bastard was going to

rub my nose in it from the grave. All his billions...and I'd get nothing.

Not that I cared.

Much, anyway.

"Sorry," Reid said. "But it'll be good to see you, bro. I've...missed you."

Truthfully, I'd missed him as well. He was my youngest brother, and he and I had been close once. Roy, who fell between us, was a classic introvert who'd spent most of his childhood in his room painting or reading. That left Reid to be my primary playmate, even though he was five years younger. Riley hadn't come around until I was eight and Reid was three.

"All right. I'll get a flight."

"I'm one step ahead of you. I'm emailing you your confirmation. Pack a bag. Your flight leaves out of Helena in three hours."

Continue reading Rebel!

A NOTE FROM HELEN

Dear Reader,

Thank you for reading *Reunited*. If you want to find out about my current backlist and future releases, please visit my website, like my Facebook page, and join my mailing list. If you're a fan, please join my Facebook street team (Hardt & Soul) to help spread the word about my books. I regularly do awesome giveaways for my street team members.

If you enjoyed the story, please take the time to leave a review. I welcome all feedback.

I wish you all the best!

Helen

Sign up for my newsletter here:

http://www.helenhardt.com/signup

ABOUT THE AUTHOR

#1 *New York Times*, #1 *USA Today*, and #1 *Wall Street Journal* bestselling author Helen Hardt's passion for the written word began with the books her mother read to her at bedtime. She wrote her first story at age six and hasn't stopped since. In addition to being an award-winning author of romantic fiction, she's a mother, an attorney, a black belt in Taekwondo, a grammar geek, an appreciator of fine red wine, and a lover of Ben and Jerry's ice cream. She writes from her home in Colorado, where she lives with her family. Helen loves to hear from readers.

Please sign up for her newsletter here:
http://www.helenhardt.com/signup
Visit her here:
http://www.helenhardt.com

Lightning Source UK Ltd.
Milton Keynes UK
UKHW042248041222
413345UK00002B/469

9 780990 746188

REUNITED

HELEN HARDT VINTAGE COLLECTION

HELEN HARDT

REUNITED

HH VINTAGE COLLECTION

Helen Hardt

HARDT & SONS ♥